Womandrakes

Hi, Aaron!

One thing!

Womandrakes

Two Stories in the German Style

Anne Sharp

To order additional copies of this book, contact:
Xlibris Corporation
1-888-7-XLIBRIS
www.Xlibris.com
Orders@Xlibris.com

THE
WOMANDRAKES

It was Lulu who came to me finally. Father, she said, why aren't I like the other girls?

You mean, not like Lola and Lorelei? I said.

No, the *other* ones. They do something I don't.

What's that? I said.

She folded her hands behind her back. I can't tell you, she said.

Well, I said, if you can't tell me I can't tell you.

Lola and Lorelei don't do it either, she murmured.

You mean *won't* do it, *can't*?

No, just *don't*.

(It was like the riddle about the explorers that find two bodies in ice, and realize they must be Adam and Eve. You have to stare through the ice at those bodies for a long time yourself before *you* see why. Finally I saw it.)

Go call your sisters, Lulu, I said.

I went out to the shed and assembled a visual aid for the little talk I was about to give. I put it in my pocket, ready to pull out at the right time. When I came back they had arrived, and assembled themselves prettily at my feet.

Girls, I began, you know you're . . . different.

Yes, said Lorelei, *we* know, we're unearthly beautiful.

I cleared my throat. That's not the only difference, I said. Perhaps Lulu has told you. . .

(They giggled.)

My jacket felt too tight; I felt my forehead bead up slightly. I won't discuss that, I said. My subject for today is . . . it's about *growing*, girls.

They drew nearer, their shifts rustling over their bare legs.

When a man dies by strangulation, I told them, there is a peculiar physiologic response that occurs at the moment of death. In his last moments, the hanged man experiences a spasmodic eruption of his masculine fluids, an . . . erotic climax. That's one of the reasons hanging's such a popular way of dying among us men. Anyway, when it happens that a man is hanged out in the open, over bare ground, out in the woods, say, or at an unpaved crossroads, at that moment when the hanged man . . . spills his seed . . . well, like any seed when it strikes fertile ground, it grows, it takes root. Little tendrils, like fetal feet, kick down in the earth, feeling around for nourishment. And little shoots reach up to catch the moisture from the soil above, and in between these little arms a little head pokes up into the sunshine, sprouting a mop of fine green floss. Do you know what they call this little man-root that grows under the gallows?

It's a mandrake, said Lulu.

So, I said. You've heard of it.

Of course, said Lola.

Then you know, I said, that a mandrake is a very precious, a very desirable thing to possess.

They're magic, aren't they? asked Lorelei. Witches have them. They use them for spells and things.

Oh, yes, I said. Well, you have to know magic before you can even get a mandrake out of the ground. Do you know how it's done? You have to go to the place where the mandrake's growing, under the gallows, at midnight, the night of a full moon. And you have to have these things with you, a piece of rope, and some soft wax, and a piece of meat, the bloodier the better, and a black dog. First you take the wax and pull it into a couple of plugs and stop up your ears with it. Then you take the rope, tie one end of it round the dog's throat, and the other round the neck of the little mandrake. Then, when you've got the dog and the mandrake tied together, you take the meat, tease the dog with it (it helps if you've starved it for a couple of days) and then throw the meat so the dog jumps after it and tugs and tears at its rope till it rips the mandrake right out of its socket. And when that happens you'd have better plugged your ears up tight with that wax, because when that mandrake comes out of the ground it shrieks a shriek so shrill it could kill you. The dog drops dead. It has to. The mandrake demands a sacrifice when it's born out of the ground; something's got to die. Better a dog than you. Now. Once you've got your mandrake, you take it home, and wash it in wine, and wrap it up in a little silk robe, and you keep it in a nice box. And this little mandrake, if you care for it carefully and treat it to its favorite wine and silk, will do wonders for you. It can make you rich. It can keep you young. But like all magical things, it can be deadly dangerous if you don't treat it the way it ought to be treated, so you'd better know just what you're doing if you're going to keep a mandrake, or a womandrake. Did you know about womandrakes? They're even rarer than mandrakes. Mandrakes, you see, are created when a man is hung by other men; it's a common enough thing. But a womandrake can only be planted by a man who hangs himself for—for purposes of love, girls. The womandrake's far more powerful than a mandrake. And you'd better be extra careful with a womandrake, because she's infinitely more deadly.

What gives the womandrake more power? asked Lulu.

A mandrake's a withered thing, I told her, a dry root, just a crude little wooden manikin, tiny enough to fit in your pocket. But a womandrake is something beautiful, blooming, it breathes, it speaks, it's like a real woman, in fact, in almost every way you can imagine. A womandrake can walk among mortal men, and not one of them will know what she really is. She herself might not even realize she is a womandrake. . . . Have you ever wondered where you come from, girls? Have you ever wondered why I always dress you in silk? Why I always have you bathe in wine?

I thought you said wine was a good astringent, said Lorelei.

It's also damn expensive, I groaned.

What are you saying, Father? snapped Lulu. That we're some sort of vegetables? That we grew in the dirt?

You think it's cleaner to grow inside a woman? I sneered.

Father! cried Lorelei.

I'm not your father! I said, you're not my seed, thank God. *This—this* is your father. (I dangled the noose in their faces.)

I don't believe it! Lulu snarled. I'm a human being, not a plant!

I seized her glossy head, squeezed its softness between my hands. Lulu, I whispered, your hair is black. Like the cap of a poison mushroom. Lola, your curls rattle in the wind like red maple leaves. And Lorelei, your hair is like the moss in the meadows where I used to chase the girls and make them tumble over—I could fall into it right now!

Lorelei screamed as if I'd hurt her—she pummeled at me with her little pink claws. Lulu caught me a good round slap on my poor old chops.

You dirty old man, said Lola, stepping away.

You womandrake, I countered, following her. You womandrake. So I should be your first victim. The horticulturist devoured by . . . whhhat he cultured. You listen to me. Understand yourselves, and when you know what you really are, what a threat you pose to the masculine world, you might at least try to control your toxicity.

Daddy! cried Lorelei (oh, she was bewitching in tears! It was all I could do not to—)

Womandrakes! I roared. Don't touch me! Your effect on me and all men is lethal! You are fatal women, all of you, and your power to destroy my sex is incalculable. Right now just looking at you, I'm getting an erection. For what you do to me—I can't be held responsible!

*   *   *

They stood over me, Lola holding the rope, Lorelei standing on my chest, Lulu with one hand on my chin, the other below the base of my skull, nodding it to and fro; yes, yes, I'm dead.

He wanted us to do this, Lorelei whispered.

Wonder if he got any fun out of it? said Lola.

Well, he doesn't look very happy to be *dead*! What'll we do, where will we go?

If we are monsters, said Lulu, we'll go to the city. We'll blend in there.

What will we do with him?

Lulu pouted. Seems to me, she said, the obvious thing would be—take a knife and cut his guts out. They're the first thing to rot. Then drag them out to the woods and feed them to the feral cats.

Okay, said Lorelei. But what about the rest?

Find the beef chart in the big white cookbook, said Lulu. Get a saw and cut him up into steaks and chops. We'll put the rest through the mincer. And we'll set up the grill and invite all the men we know for a cookout. We'll give them lots of beer; they'll eat anything we give them. Except the eyes and gristle; we'll roll them into a ball and hang it out for the sparrows and squirrels. And we'll grind his bones to make our bread.

We'll have nice hard nails with all that protein, said Lola.

We'll paint them blood red, Lulu smiled.

That's very fashionable in the city, chirruped Lorelei.

*   *   *

Lola was first to rise the next morning. She borrowed Lulu's best kid shoes, put on her new brown frock, brushed out her crisp autumn-leaf hair. Then, humming scales all the way (she was trying to teach herself to sing on pitch), she trotted the two miles into town, to the boys' Gymnasium. Curtsied to the secretary:

Please, can you tell me where my father's classroom is? Thank you (prettily).

She took the stairs one at a time, in a very grown ladylike manner. The boys gathered underneath, but look up as they might they couldn't see anything. Of course not; that's why she wore brown, it makes a *shadow*.

The boys were already assembled, squiggling and sniggering behind their desks, but not yet utterly wild, still anticipating the entrance of their old master (I was then being tugged out of the icebox by a sleepy Lorelei, in preparation for being pounded into schnitzels). When Lola came in, it positively made my soon-to-be-cutleted self turn like a top, right under Lorelei's astonished hands: the sounds those naughty ex-pupils of mine made! the poundings those desks took! not to mention the strain endured by those twenty adolescent pairs of underdrawers! as Lola walked up before the blackboard, smiling, and leaned against the rostrum.

All right, all right, boys! (my Lulu drawled at them). Listen! I'm here to tell you the Schoolmaster won't be coming in to teach your class anymore. He got himself into an accident playing hangman. Anyway, you can all go home. Don't you want to go? You're just sitting there gawking? Well hello to you too (she cooed to one of the naughtiest, nastiest catcallers). So, now! Take out your copybooks. We'll have class. My way.

(She arranged her various bumps and valleys along the edge of my desk.)

I'm going to read to you a poem, she told them, and I want you to write it down as I say it word for word. After you've taken it down I'm going to explain what it means. You've got your pencils out? Good little boys. Now write down this title. The title is, "My Hole." That's the poem, "My Hole." You think that's funny? H'm. Here's the poem. Get your pens ready. This is the poem.

My hole is little and round.
It goes deep deep in the ground.
I used to live there
And only my hair
Was accustomed to shining in sun.
My body was stuck in the black
With worms crawling deep in the crack
Of mother the earth
And so she gave birth
And now I stand firmly on top of the earth, breathing air,
But I still have a hole, little dark deep, right down there.

Got that? Who can tell me what metrical scheme this poem is written in? You over there, can you? Oh come on boys, you had a whole unit in poetics last semester. You there, what are you looking at? That doesn't look like a poem to me. Give it here. Ohh. You dirty little—What faraway friend sent you *this* post-card? You know who this is? Yes, this young person in the black mask and stockings. This is my sister Lulu. You can forget about it, little fellow. You can't afford her. To get that one it takes quite a sacrifice,

And she flounced out of the room—*with* the post card. They groaned with regret—I think they're still groaning.

* * *

This is what Lulu wrote on the back of the postcard.

I'll tell you something you've always wanted to know. Something you always suspected.

We're not like you. And the more young we are, the less like you we are. We don't want what you want. You see, we're built differently. Obviously. But I mean, differently. It makes us not want what you want. See when we want, it's not a want where you have to go in. We already are in. Made that way. We are so sensitive. You just touch us in the right place, and—you said where. Sorry, there's no one right place. Not like you, where you just put your hand in your pants and it's right there. On us it can be anywhere. You don't know. We don't know either. Could be the little place here where I just go like—or here—kind of hurts, it's really sensitive tonight—or right here under my diaphragm—you just don't know—you could put a finger right there and we go—ow.

See we're tuned up so high, we're wound to such a tight ticking place that we feel harder. You're so mechanical and limited—you're either on or you're off, you're hard or you're soft, you can't imagine this kind of good that lasts this long and's so easy—and it goes on for hours—I feel good all night long. All by myself, look daddy no hands. Frustration, I don't know what it means. I throb all over. And it's never over. I don't need you, see. But I'll let you come over sometime, when I say you can, and I'll let you watch me.

*   *   *

The barbecue was a great success, by the way. My dear girls decamped that evening with their hatboxes and valises, leaving a townful of young men satisfied in almost every way, and a stink of smoke that hung over the village for a week.

*   *   *

What an adventure for my little Womandrakes! In all their lives, they'd barely been out of sight of the village crossroads where they were bred, and now they were out in the great wide world!

When they first stepped inside the gates of the city, the first thing they saw was a magnificent black-lettered sign with the royal proclamation: ALL VIRGINS REPORT TO THE MARKET SQUARE AT NOON. Lulu discreetly went ahead to find lodgings; Lola and Lorelei scampered towards the center of town, naturally not wanting to miss whatever it was they mustn't miss, by order of the King.

It was impossible to find the end of the line. The city girls, envious of their obviously superior looks, pointed them in the wrong direction so many times they finally simply dug into the crush, and refused to move. The crowd was immense, ridiculously so. The fresh young girls, the doubled-over crones, the babies so weary they were oblivious to all the high-pitched noise; the King hadn't bothered to specify what *age* of virgins he wanted. It was a wonder the virgin men hadn't shown up too (or could it be there were NO virgin men?)

Lola was casual, bemused. She threw back her head, shimmied her curls. Because of *them*, she'd be out of the running. What King would have a girl, however exquisite, with such obvious hell in her hair? To keep herself as well as her fellow unviolated females amused, she began to sing, in that hoarse, sweet voice:

Mister, have you met the Woman Drake?
Oh, be careful of that girl, for pity's sake!

By the end of the day, every virtuous girl and woman in the city would know that song, as would the King's physician and other royal servants who did duty in the examination tent, and every man and boy who trolled round the marketplace to feast his fancy on the fresh femininity herded there. Think of having a chance to have a song *you* wrote become popular so quickly! So Lola hardly felt the day in the marketplace had been in vain, as she dandled her hips jauntily along the waiting line under the hot sun and gave tongue to the song of her sisterhood.

The older ladies and little girls were turned away at the door of the tent; after a while, a page was sent round to tell these unsuitables they could go home, before they crumpled needlessly in the heat. Well, that was all right for them; but the girls who did go into the tent, Lola noticed, came out looking less than happy to go home, or go anywhere except to the deepest part of the river and put themselves at the bottom of it. Many sobbed, had various facial fluids streaming down their cheeks and chins. One, wailing hysterically, ran out of the tent wearing nothing but an undershirt. What are those crazy men doing? Lola wondered. They'd better be careful with those poking fingers, or how are they going to convince the King there were no virgins in this town after all?

When her turn came, she simply went in, unfastened her dress, dropped it; gave them time to form the picture they would use that night while visiting with their sweethearts or stroking their swans; then replaced the garment on her shoulders and sauntered out the back way, humming, *Mister, have you met the Woman Drake?* She then leaned against a tent pole, lit a cigarette and listened to the reactions, already burbling, over her sister Lorelei, who had come in right behind her. Sweet Lorelei, chattering innocently provocative questions as the men probed and smoothed her, felt and peered at every area, just to be sure.

Finally, not a moment after Lola suspected it would be, and actually several moments beforehand, the call went up: Go home, you virgins! Tell everybody, we have found your new Queen!

And what a bargain the King's getting! thought Lola. A wife who doesn't bleed, from month to month and moon to moon! And two sisters-in-law who'll make the most lovely ladies in waiting. But you'll wait for *us*, crown head, if a trio's what you've got in mind. Lulu and I've got other plans.

*   *   *

Lola and Lulu couldn't have lived in the castle, anyway; it would have restricted their movements. Lola preferred to be near the entertainment district, where she worked; and Lulu by then had her own little jewelbox lodgings, purchased for her by a friendly protector. Another reason for not living with Queen Lorelei in her little Trianon was: it was haunted!

They noticed it the first time Lorelei invited them there to show them her new jewels. Something stirring among the draperies, shifting in silouhette through the layers of silk that swagged through the rooms; the rather Bedouin tastes of that boudoir's former tenant, the old Queen.

Cautiously, not to frighten the ghost, they stalked it down. But it wasn't a dead thing; it was warm, and soft in the unsatisfying way old skin is, giving no resistance. It was the old Queen. In the excitement of rushing to grant the King's wish for a new one, the courtiers and lackeys must have completely forgotten to put out the old one. She had been beautiful once, even a very young beauty could see that. She seemed strange, sleepy but not weary. Unbidden, she spoke:

Little bunny, she crooned.

The girls drew closer, fascinated by the softness of that voice, coming from that folded old throat.

Velvet and straw, sighed the old Queen, singsong. Toy bunny. Sick little boy had her. She was in his bed every night. He'd hold her, chew her, drool on her. Till she was all worn out and her stuffing was coming out. He said you're not pretty and threw her out. *But.* When the trash man came and lifted up the lid on the can, something happened to bunny: suddenly she wasn't cloth and straw anymore, she was all fur and muscle! and her heart beat hard, her fur bristled and her whiskers twitched, and before the man could dump her in that stinky heap in the back of his truck she hopped out and ran away! And so you see, after they stop sleeping with you, you become real.

She was adorable! Lorelei thought: I need a lady's maid.

*   *   *

All men yearn for the perfect woman; this is no secret. And women also dream of an ideal woman. Every one of us dreams incessantly of this unreal female.

She is immortal. She is ageless. She is physical perfection, it goes without saying. But what is paramount about this matchless feminine specimen is that she is impervious to pain. She is immaculately self-protective; she does no wrong to herself, and most important, no man alive can harm her in any way. Not that she cannot feel pain; her senses are exquisite. But this woman, in her perfection, can deflect all malice, all thoughtlessness or neglect or intended humiliation, so that it strikes not her, but the very person who would harm her. Her perfection then is its own defense. She doesn't need to work or strive as normal women do; her preternatural beauty and ruthlessness can obtain her all material things she might desire. A force field of absolute science fiction invincibility surrounds her. In this she is like no human woman we have ever known. Never broken, never pitiful, never violated, never used up. No one need ever be ashamed to look at what she is. All men long for this woman. All women wonder why they are not like her. They might as well wonder why they aren't unicorns. The womandrake is just as rare. And you men who want a womandrake, you might as well try to embrace a manticore. A yeti. A plesiosaurus in Loch Ness. But it's in our nature, this erotomaniacal pursuit of the cryptozoological, we must pursue these fabulous creatures, even to our deaths. We cannot help ourselves. After all, *we* are not womandrakes. We can only marvel at the breathless possibility of such unpossessable inhumanity.

*   *   *

Bunny lady, cooed Lorelei, tell us how you met the King.

All right, the old Queen said, smiling indulgently, but sit still. I can't fix your diadem straight while you're fidgeting like that! I met His Highness at my debutante ball; he was just a prince then. How we waltzed! I was wearing a pair of four-inch heels. Each heel was about as big around as a soda straw. I caught one on the hem of my train and went down like *that*: my ankle twisted like *this*. I was laid up for weeks. He liked that. I was at his mercy then.

She told me a word for what we are today, Lorelei told the others. It was femme fatale. What did you say it means, Bun?

Fatal woman, your Majesty. A fatal woman who lures men to their doom.

Men deserve to be doomed, muttered Lulu. I hate old men. They smell. Always trying to rub off their wrinkles on you.

It satisfies me there's girls like you in the world, said the Bun, with a motherly smile. Ruination girls. You ruined me, but someone would have done it eventually.

Oh, Bunbun, I didn't want the King, pouted Lorelei. He made me go in that stupid tent and get picked to be Queen.

It was good that you did, and you were a good choice for Queen. You are the most beautiful virgin in the city.

You mean I *was.*

Oh, how was that, by the way?

Pretty scary. That suction pump thing.

Oh, no.

Yeah, I got in the bed and he's all tucked in, proud of himself—pull back the covers—nothing. He's so embarrassed, he opens the drawer, takes out this thing like a cross between a cookie press and a douche bag, and he takes this wobbly little piece of liverwurst he's got, and pokes it in there, and goes *skwook skwook skwook—*

I'm glad I'm out of that.

Did he ever—

Oh, no no. I had him when he could still go under his own power.

So, what is a fatal woman, Bun? persisted Lulu.

Well, you are, kitten.

So you say. But what are a fatal woman's, I don't know, attributes? What makes her so fatal?

Well. Remember last week when you threw that vaseful of roses in Jim Felch's face and he got a thorn in his eye?

Oh, yeah, it made him cry! chuckled Lulu. But he was so mean, *he asked for it!*

Well, they all ask for it, but they don't think they're going to get it. Most of the time they don't. You'd be surprised.

But why?

Queen Bun smiled, set down the platinum brush in her lap.

You've heard of love, girls, she told them. Love is what men feel when they're sexually aroused. And it's what women feel when they're afraid of being thrown out in the street. It's a dangerous emotion. Just be glad you can't have it. You'll be much safer. And richer! And less visits to the gynecologist. All around better. Now Lulu, are you going to take us for a ride in that new car Jim gave you?

Which new car? Lulu smirked, rattling her pearls provocatively. The green one or the gold one?

*   *   *

An experiment was undertaken, back in the days when photography was done not with film, but with huge photographic plates made of glass. On each of the photographic plates used in the experiment—there were a hundred of them—there was a picture of a single human face. And each face on each of these plates was put one on top of the other, in a monumental stack, and exposed to the sun, the sun being the only developer powerful enough to penetrate that stack of plates, casting a composite image made of all those faces laid one on top of the other onto a raw, undeveloped photo plate at the very bottom. And when that new plate was developed, that plate in which the faces of a hundred human souls were blurred together into one composite face, it was the most beautiful face anyone had ever seen. Featureless. Impersonal. The image of ideal desire.

A beautiful face should be like a cinema screen. Blank, so that the beholder can project his fantasies onto it, without any blots or creases. An old face can only be ugly. Only the young, clear face of a beautiful woman, unsullied by thought or emotion, can truly tempt a man. We all know the enticement of fresh snow on a new morning. Or a patch of wet concrete pavement, smooth and unmarked, when there's a stick in your hand and nobody looking.

But beware of a woman who bathes in wine and wears only silk. You know what she is!

*　*　*

Lulu paddled indolently in her tub, scudding down so the scarlet tide crept over her breasts (just the right fit for her slender chest—enough to fill a champagne glass, with not a bite wasted). Jim was there to pass her the sponge.

Is that blood in your bathwater, Lulu? he muttered. What are you doing, cleaning up after your latest kill? What is that in there, wine?

You drink too much, Jim.

It's my best beaujolais, he moaned. My god, you'll ruin me.

She smirked. Better than you ruining me, she said.

He turned his head so she wouldn't see what his eyes were doing.

You weren't there last night, he said. Where were you? You come and go like a ghost.

(For a moment—she did look a little scared, didn't she?)

You've never seen a ghost in your life, she muttered.

When I realized you weren't coming last night, he said, I went a little crazy. I went out in the street. I ended up down by the river.

Obviously you didn't jump in.

I ended up in some nightclub. It was weird. Lola was working there. I watched her show.

Shame on you.

She's really good, you know.

I wouldn't know.

You've never seen her act?

I never go in those places.

Well, I've seen you pinned up in some pretty raunchy places.
It wasn't me, it was pictures of me. It's not the same.

Yeah, well you show about all there is to show of yourself,
outside of turning yourself inside out in front of those cameras.
Letting anybody who wants to take a look. But that's all you ever
give, isn't it? Just a look.

(Lulu was humming that new song, Lola's song; now I know
what that tune is, she thought. It's "Wedding Day at Troldhaugen.")

Lulu, said Jim, I need sex.

Buy it, she replied.

I don't have any money left.

Make some.

I'm broke, he said, breaking down. You did this to me. You
vampire.

Rising, she dabbed the beaujolais from her breasts. No, she
said, who's the vampire here, *old man*?

I need you. Doesn't that mean anything to you? I have nothing left. Give me something, some part of you! I love you!

What do you mean by *love*?

And Jim, finding no reply, reaching past her ruby-moist thighs,
dipped cupped hands into the tub, lowered his face like a beast
at the edge of a brook.

*   *   *

Mister, have you met the Woman Drake?
Oh, be careful of that girl, for pity's sake!
She'll wrap herself around you like a snake
And she'll take you, man, for all that she can take!

You think she'll make a pretty little pet
And you think she's got a pretty little set
But all the time she's reeling in her net
And she'll get you, yes, for all that she can get!

Tell me, have you met the Woman Drake?
Just avoid her, boy, you'll make a bad mistake!
She'll wrap herself around you like a snake
And she'll take you, man, for all that she can take!

*   *   *

To celebrate Lola's recording contract, Lorelei brought over champagne from the King's cellar. They used it to make their favorite bubbly ice cream sodas. Staggering Jim, smelling like a specimen bottle, held up Lola's shoe (his portion of the refreshment was inside it) and made the toast (with rather clumsily formed labials):

To lovely Lola. And her three weird sisters. *Two* weird sisters. And now, he said, I'll be sick.

No, no, not in my shoe! said Lola. Get out, go do it on your own shoes.

She turned to Lulu. You've destroyed that man, she said. I'm so proud of you.

And the young Queen sighed:

You know, sometimes I wish we hadn't killed Father. There's a lot I'd like to ask him right now about us. Like how we're supposed to have babies. I guess we can't do it the regular way.

What? squeaked Lulu.

I think it's part of us being not real women. The royal surgeon looked me over yesterday and told me that some things are missing off my body. I mean, I have everything on the outside that a woman could possibly want. But inside me, around here, there's supposed to be stuff that makes babies, and . . . I don't have any of it.

That's what my doctor told me, too, Lola drawled. He said: you are basically a beautiful tunnel leading nowhere.

That's a terrible thing to say! cried Lorelei.

You should have seen where I put his speculum, Lola smiled. So none of us can have babies?

Not in the usual way.

So if we can't have them, where do little womandrakes come from?

Hey! Father told us! Remember? They grow in the ground! That's where we grew! Under the hanged men!

That's right! The men who've hanged themselves for love!

Which in male terms must mean something disgusting.

Of course! They do it for the thrill! And that's what makes a womandrake!

So you want a little baby, Lorelei?

Yes, well, I guess it's kind of expected of me.

The king, eh? Oh, it's true, he likes his babies. You'd better give him one or—

(Lola made the universal throat-slitting signal.)

Yeah. I know it wouldn't kill me or anything, but I'd hate to go through life without a head.

Oh, it would probably grow back.

But I like *this* one.

Anyway, it's academic. Lorelei will have a baby, and we're going to get it. I'm trying to remember what Father said about how you get a womandrake out of the ground. He said you had to pull it out at midnight on a full moon. And you need a dog, right?

Yes, Lulu purred. A dog to sacrifice. And I think I have just the right dog in mind.

* * *

Item found by Queen Lorelei in her morning gazette:

Fifty-five-year-old businessman Heinz Beckmann was found dead yesterday in a wooded area near his home in Bittenburg.

Beckmann was discovered with a belt around his neck. Police have ruled out foul play. The coroner ruled the probable cause of death to be autoerotic asphyxia.

(Shrieks of joy trembled the draperies of the royal bedchamber.)

*   *   *

Hand in hand, the sisters tripped through the forest.

Here! It was right here! exclaimed Queen Lorelei.

Of course it was! said Lola. He hung himself on that tree, from this branch.

That's a little low to hang a noose on, isn't it? said Lulu.

Lola stooped down. Not if you're lying down, she said . . . and you want that little log there to prop up your arm so your wrist won't get tired.

I hope before he died he managed to spill a little spume around here, said Lulu.

I'm sure he did, replied Lola, and lucky for us—unless he was one of those worthless bastards with a lousy sperm count. Look! This is it! Oh, look at its little baby hair! A womandrake!

What was it Father said? said Lorelei. You have to pull it out of the ground at midnight. He said it screamed.

Yes, said Lola, that's why you have a dog to do it, so the dog drops dead instead of you.

I don't believe it, said Lorelei. That sounds like one of his stories. Only a man would be that afraid of a baby's scream. Oh, I've always wanted a little girl!

Well, you'll have one soon, said Lulu. And we'll help you, Lorelei. I'll have Jim buy me this whole piece of land, and we'll build a fence around it so no one can disturb her while she's growing.

Can we get an electric fence? said Lorelei.

Sure, said Lola. That would be fun.

Lorelei danced and clapped her hands. I'll have the king's vintners press a special vintage of new wine for her christening bath, she said. I'll have my best silkworms weave a bunting for her.

She kissed her sisters.

Did you ever think anything this beautiful could come from a *man*? she cried.

*   *   *

Listen to me. All beauty is despicable.

*   *   *

A band of black velvet, tied over Lulu's eyes, cut roughly into her creamy skin, made her stumble as she moved where Jim led her, made her . . . tantalizing beyond description. The floor felt like parquet; there was music. Are we there, Jim? she whispered. Where are we?

You'll never know, he murmured, lowering her shoulder straps.

No! Don't do that! You want them to see us?

Who?

The musicians! (A trio; they were playing Grieg.)

They're all wearing blindfolds, just like yours, Jim assured her. We're perfectly alone, Lulu.

I don't believe you.

Jim slapped her playfully. Half the men in the world know your yin-yang as well as they know your face, he told her, and you're worried about flashing a couple of fiddle players. They can't see you, Lulu. What's more they can't hear you. I've stopped their ears up with wax. Don't believe me? Try screaming. Go ahead. Scream. . .

Well, you can't now, can you? he susurrated. Not with a broken throat. (He rubbed his lips along it.) Lululululu. You were all muscle and ooze, like an eel, I could never get hold of you. But now . . . I like you limp like this, like an eel . . . you taste even better . . . let's see if you've tightened up. . .

Then he screamed; she'd sat up.

Ahh. Ahaha, he laughed. Lulu. I thought I'd killed you.

You can't.

(She pulled off her blindfold.)

I can't die, she said.

*   *   *

So, the old Queen chirruped, the King's suction pumps must have worked! Here, Your Majesty, I made something for the little prince.

Oh, thank you, Bunny! said the new Queen. But it's not going to be a prince; it's a princess.

How wonderful! When's it due?

We're expecting her the night of the next full moon.

So soon! You don't look that far along.

Oh, giggled Queen Lorelei, patting the rather oddly-shaped protrusion under her robe, it's because I'm so thin. Really skinny women don't show. Even up till the last minute. How many babies have you had, Bun?

Seven.

Seven! No wonder you're so stretched out looking. I'm amazed you can walk. Did it hurt when you had them?

Oh, the first time it was so bad I wanted to jump out the window.

And you did it SEVEN TIMES?

Mm, there's a process of forgetting, you know, after it's all over. Anyway, the King likes his babies.

He was so happy when I told him.

Well, we were all so relieved, I can tell you. We were worried there for a while maybe there was something wrong, maybe you couldn't, and then oh God! Remember what happened to the wife before me!

(Both Queens touched their throats.)

Actually, that's probably more pleasant than having a baby in the long run, it's over faster anyway. But then you don't get the rewards. When you see that little face looking up at you. . .

(But then Lorelei, reaching for her powder-puff, let the pillow slip; it fell to her feet.)

Oh, your majesty, breathed the old Queen. *Oh*. Then. Where

are you going to get that baby from? You're not going to KILL
anybody?

$$* \quad * \quad *$$

JIM FELCH'S MANIFESTO
(nailed to the door of the City Parfumerie)
Women of the world! This is the MAN speaking! We, the MAN,
hold these truths to be self-evident, that all men are created in
the image of GOD, with superior strength and natural endow-
ments that have made us the rightful possessors of this earth!
You will no longer deny us this birthright, you who are weak
and are our inferiors, who were put on this earth to be used by
us as the BITCH animals you are!
We refuse anymore to share our money and material goods with
women. Therefore we reject the obsolete institution of "mar-
riage," and its reverse corollary, "divorce." Monogamy is a life-
draining perversion and we reject it as living death!
Since women are the ones that bring biological replicants into
the world, it follows that they should assume the responsibility of
raising, educating, and paying for their own biological
replicants. If they want the help of men in making or taking
care of their replicants, they can pay us for the privilege!
It is not only unnatural for a man to be denied sex, it is danger-
ous! It's been proven by science, and by our own individual
bodies, that for physical and mental health, men need regular
sex. All men at all times! We will no longer be denied sex for any
reason, period!
We abolish woman-made rules about sex. We refuse to acknowl-
edge phony, anti-sex concepts such as "rape," "statutory rape,"
and "child abuse." No law and no woman has the right to deny
a man his right to choose his own sex partner. There is only one
natural law when it comes to sex: Let the erection make the
selection!

We hereby issue a death sentence for censors of language, images, and real life. You will never again deny us our right to express our manhood in pictures, in words, or in deed. You— woman—WILL FORBID US NOTHING FROM NOW ON!

(It seems they found him face down in the market square in the morning, and carried him back to the Trianon, on the Queen's orders.)

*   *   *

Past time for you to be born, little one, murmured Lorelei, stroking the little floss-head. You're ripe and ready, like I was. All right! How's the dog?

He's crying for another whiskey, said Lola.

Give him the whole bottle, replied Lulu. How does the little one look?

Like a princess! smiled Lola.

You'd think the King would want a boy child, said Lulu.

Lorelei lifted her chin. The King has seen the error of his ways, she announced.

Lulu cocked her head. Anybody bring the wax? she asked.

The wax for the ear plugs! moaned Lorelei. Oh, no!

We could put our fingers in our ears, Lola shrugged.

Would that work? said Lorelei hopefully.

Well, we can try, said Lola. Tighten that rope on him. Do we put the knot under the ear or at the base of the neck?

I don't know, said Lorelei, whatever looks good to you.

Let's do it, said Lola. Okay, Lulu.

(Lulu opened her silken robe, revealing her body; Jim did what any man would do. The noose snapped his neck back; he began to die. But then, a deafening SHRIEK:)

JIM!

(Hippety-hopp came Bunny.)

Jim! cried the old Queen. What did they do to you? You're lucky you didn't tear your head off!

Get away from me, snarled Jim. You're old and ugly.

Come on, Jim, the old Queen urged.

I want to stay with them, he whined.

She snatched the rope, rounded on the girls. You . . . you *womandrakes*, she said. You're not like any real woman who's ever lived. You're nothing but a nightmare from a sick mind. I'm glad I'm not one of *you*.

People say things like that, said Lulu airily. Like they say they're glad they're not going to live forever.

I keep forgetting you're not human, whispered Bun. You're not even animal, you're vegetable. If I buried you in the ground, I guess you'd just keep on growing.

If I buried *you*, piped Lulu, I guess you'd just *rot*.

(Sighing, the old Queen led the whining "dog" away.)

Bye, bunny, whispered Lorelei.

Well, there goes our dog, said Lola.

But the little one! cried Lorelei. She can't just stay in the ground! We've got to get her out!

We will get her out, said Lola.

(Tenderly, she tied her sash round the little neck.)

What happens if we die? said Lorelei tremulously.

Lulu shrugged. Some man will come along and take her home with him, she said.

(As they pulled, something like screaming metal stabbed their ears; they fell to the earth, not breathing. But then, in truth, they had never truly breathed.)

Are we dead? asked Lorelei.

How can you tell? said Lulu.

I don't care if I am dead, Lorelei said, sitting up. I feel fine.

Look! said Lola, trembling with joy, cradling the little thing in her arms.

Oh! cried the new Mama Queen, let *me* hold her!

Oh, look at the little hands! cooed Lola.

She looks like you, Lola! said Lorelei.

I thought she was yours, Lorelei, smiled Lola.

She's *ours*, said Lorelei proudly. Hey. Did you feel anything when she came out?

Not a thing, said Lulu. Did you?

No, said Lola, I didn't hear anything. I didn't feel any pain.

And we didn't need a dog after all, said Lorelei. Nobody had to die. Who told us that lie?

He did. (Meaning me.)

Figures, said Lulu, pooching her lips.

So it was easy, smiled Lorelei. And she's beautiful. Painless. Painless. I'm glad I'm not a real woman.

Me too! Lola grinned.

Me too, sighed Lulu, nibbling at her diamonds.

VERLUST

For Greta

Preface

She wasn't beautiful, but that didn't matter. The problem of looks is different for an actress than for an ordinary woman. The most exquisite face may fade into plainness under stage paint and hot, hard lights, while grotesqueness bordering on deformity can be made divine by the whimsical lens of the cinema-eye.

People were always astonished to see her "in life," on the street or at a reception, away from the carefully chosen illusory settings in which she professionally exhibited herself. She was so *little*, with her startlingly large head like a child's, exaggerated features and huge, almost frighteningly eloquent eyes. She was made to be stared at; she *made* you look at her. There was no other possible destiny for her than to mold the imaginations of men.

She took her mission too seriously to play the publicity game, testily shaking off those obligatory remoras of the star fish, the Press Agents. Nor would she allow excavations into her past; she considered herself an exhibit in a locked case, and that was that! But in this respect she did herself a disservice, I think. The lives of actors and politicians are like the liver of Prometheus. They may scream a little when a bite's taken out, but later you'll notice, they're not *missing* anything. What we the public gain, however, from learning about the real lives of our matinee idols is something very necessary in a random, phantom-fed life—a

touch of something real, the human endeavor and meaning behind these synthetic dreams we feed on.

Nevertheless, this perverse look-at-me-don't-look Godiva ride
of hers worked in her favor, giving her at times an almost oneiric
aura of mystery. Whenever anyone approached her with questions about her early life, before fame, she gave the same
exasperating response. Drawing down her baroquely dimpled
chin and raising hooded lids, she'd murmur in that darkling voice:
"I'll tell you how I got to be what I am. . . .

"I was very young and times were desperate. We lost Father
in the 'flu epidemic. Then the night they took Mother away, I was
thrown out on the street with nothing but the dress on my back
and a bit of bread and three pennies clutched in my hand.

"I sat on the curb—no one looked at me. Finally an old skinny
dog came and lay down at my feet. He was so badly starved I
could see his bones, so I took the little crust of bread I had and
fed it to him. Poor thing, why shouldn't he have it? I thought.
After all, I've still got three whole pennies left and my woolen
dress to keep me warm tonight. I had no shoes and my bare feet
were freezing, but I danced down the street and that kept me
from feeling so numb.

"Then I met a beggar woman with two little boys. They looked
so sad, I gave each of them a penny to make them smile. I'll
never miss those pennies, I thought, not when I have my dress
my mother made for me, keeping me warm on this freezing night.

"Then I saw a little girl. She was trembling, and blue with the
cold, ready to give up the ghost. All she had on was a little worn-
out cotton shift, more holes than fabric. You could see her little
body right through it. So I took off my dress and wrapped her up
in it, and soon she was warm and pink again. I thought, well, it
doesn't matter if I go naked. I won't get cold if I keep moving,
and no one will see me if I go off to the woods.

"The forest felt good to me, after the chill of the city. The
bare earth was warmer than the pavement, and the trees covered
me with their branches, so I felt safe. I stopped to rest in a clear-

ing, where I could look through the branches to the sky where the stars shone like diamonds on black velvet.

"One star was brighter than the others. It shivered in its space, as if trying to shake itself loose. And then, *pop*! it fell down! straight through the branches above me, and *PLOP*! it fell right at my feet!

"I looked up again—there was another star, tumbling down— and another, and another! snapping through the branches, bouncing on my toes! *ouch*!

"I knelt and touched the little stars. They were real all right. I picked one up and the other stars moved along with it, as if they'd been woven together in one glistening web of reflected light. I held the star-fabric up, and could see that it was formed in the shape of a lady's dress, a dazzling gown no queen on earth could hope to possess the like of. I slipped it on. It fit! perfectly!

"Now in my gown of stars, I was certainly fit to be seen again. So I went back to the city. Everyone I met looked as if they saw not me as I was before, but a woman transfigured, as though I were a dream, an angel. And I wanted them to see me—I had to be seen! So I went to the place where we all go to see and be seen, which is the theater.

"I wore my star dress to my first audition. I got the part. And since then, my life has been very different, as you know. I still have that dress. I wear it sometimes. But only on the stage. Some-times I wear it under my costume, sometimes I wear it alone. And when I do have it on, you'll know it. Oh, yes, you'll know!"

That was the story she told everyone. Now, the truth.

Chapter 1

Dora and Elise loved each other and always had. Closer than sisters, more tender than friends, they were always together, arm in arm, laughing and kissing. What was the harm in it? They were just little girls.

Elise's house was the first place Dora was allowed to go to by herself, and she was such a frequent visitor there that she was excused the usual obligations of ringing the doorbell or waiting for an invitation before joining the family at the dinner table. Nobody minded, she never got in the way. With all the people constantly swarming through Elise's house, one little Dora was barely noticed, which was all right with her. In the house where Dora lived she often went unseen.

From an early age the two little girls seemed more than playmates, growing together in shared thought and action like changeling twins. But in form and temperament they were far from identical. Where Dora was dainty and pale as a picture book fairy maiden, Elise was dark, robust and well-muscled, with thick hair and great, glittery eyes like an animal, given to sudden quick movements and strange, unexpected utterances. The weird richness of her voice, never really the voice of a child, hardly changed its deep, quietly commanding timbre as she grew into womanhood. It was the inborn asset of a creature meant to fend for herself early and well.

Elise (or Elsie, as she'd been known before rechristening herself with the more gracious Elise) always seemed like an intruder in her mother's house, scampering around and under the feet of her half-brothers and the other boarders. She was too nervous and shy to make a pet of, but didn't take bullying, either. Mother seemed rather in awe of her. It wasn't easy to love a child of such wild ingenuity. When little Elise would come home suffering from some schoolyard insult occasioned by her arrogant strangeness, Mother would soothe and caress her and tell her how wrong they were.

Elise was no beauty, but not unpleasant to look at, and Mother knew just the ways to twine up her thick braids, and just the colors and fabrics and bits of ribbon and smocking to make her youngest a treat to the eye. Mother had a flair for fashion in good taste—before her first marriage, she'd been an apprentice to the best milliner in the city—and from early on Elise had the sense to serve as willing apprentice as Mother plied her scissors and thimble and sewing machine, mending socks, hemming linen, stitching the ingeniously tailored seams that made Mother and her boys and little daughter the most handsomely turned-out family in the neighborhood. Mother always said that if Elise's life should take a less fortunate course than she deserved she could make a fine living as a ladies' draper. Indeed, the skill did serve her well by way of emergency costume repair, and more than once her needle rescued Broadway's legendary opening night talisman, the Gypsy Robe, from untimely collapse.

In the classroom little Elise was a fitful scholar. If the subject interested her, she took top marks. If not, she yawned and drew exotic fauna in her copybook. She liked home economics and chemistry, finding them much the same in practice. Algebra, on the other hand, made her want to scream, and so did English, except for when they gave you something good to read. But as with so many of the great, her true education occurred outside the classroom, and to her, befittingly, it came through the proscenium.

*　　*　　*

Realizing you are going to die someday is hard for any child. It was a particularly terrible revelation for Elise. She was six years old when it came over her and God knows what brought it on. She was healthy, everyone that she knew was in reasonable condition, and it was the middle of the sweetest summer day anyone could remember. Still she hid up in her room and wept until her brother Elmer came in to comfort her. Hearing what the matter was, he was very interested, as he had just been reading up on it.

"Of course you're scared," Elmer said. "It's nature. Out of all the living things, human beings are the only ones who know they're going to die. Did you know that? 'S true. That's why you're a superior animal."

Having gone through both his and her own handkerchiefs, Elise gratefully used the shirtsleeve he offered her.

"I know it doesn't feel like it now," Elmer told her, "but it really is good to be afraid to die. You know how we have to keep dodging squirrels when we're out in the car? Cause they don't have the brains to stay out of the road. But *you* do, you know, because you're more highly evolved. Being scared lets you know you're in trouble. It also makes your brains work faster, so you can get out of trouble.

"Nobody knows what happens after we die, that's the truth. Because nobody's figured out how to get to where you go after you die, and then come back alive. Nobody even knows where it is, that bourne from which no traveler returns—that's what Shakespeare called it. But this is the twentieth century, and we know so much now about the planets, and atoms, and electricity, and radio waves. We've got laboratories, and moving picture cameras, and maybe someday we'll fix it so we'll all be able to see for ourselves what it's going to be like when we die. So we'll never have to be scared again."

A smile trembled on Elise's mouth.

"That's right! You're lucky, being your age in a time like this. You're going to live through things no one's ever seen before."

That afternoon Elmer took her down to the Odeon, not to see the afterlife, which unfortunately hadn't been filmed yet, but for the new Max Linder movie. Elise had never seen an actor nor even the inside of a theatre, and to be in the finest motion picture palace in town overwhelmed her senses: the scratchy velvet and dry ice-cooled air against her arms, the sweet jelly candy sticking to her teeth, the swell of the orchestra, the eye-smarting dazzle of the screen. It was there in that great dark cavern of plush and gilded plaster that her entire life took shape.

In that moment, her little self still possessed by the deepest of animal terrors (despite the jujubes and Elmer's warm hand over hers), Elise sat in rapt contemplation of the great pantomimist Linder. Gazing at that great silver sprite, half-man, half-light on paper, the child who became the artist came to know the sacred rites of Thespis, which enable humankind to sanely embrace its mortal situation. "With death" is as we know the highest accolade the Spanish can bestow on the performing artist, and thereafter Elise—an American girl in the American century—was with death.

*   *   *

Another bitter understanding would rule Elise's life, but that came into play months before she was born. It concerned the death of love.

As a young girl Elise's mother had married a good, hard-working Bavarian who gave her five sons, but before they were grown he died in the influenza epidemic. The widow was still a fine strong woman, so an alert Scotsman snapped her up and took her and her young family to live on his farm out in the country, with its acres of apple and pear trees.

This arrangement only lasted a few weeks. The Scot turned out to be very strange, and none of his stepsons could stand him. Mother moved back into the house her first husband had built for her, which fortunately hadn't been sold yet, arranged to take in boarders from the local machinist's guild as a way to feed herself and the boys, and waited until Elise was born to get her divorce.

Left alone on his property in the middle of nowhere, Elise's father was inconsolable. He refused to tend his orchards. When the fruits came in fall, he let them hang and split the weakened branches. But Mother was a provident woman and saw that her young never wanted for apples or anything.

Elise arrived three days after Christmas. Though her father remained on the outskirts of her life, she barely felt the lack of him, the house was otherwise so full of men. Pretty decent men, but noisy and grubby and EVERYWHERE, thundering around overhead, underfoot—it drove her crazy. "See if *I* ever marry," she told Dora.

Dora had known her own father fairly well. He was a merchant sailor who had usually come by to stay when his ship was docked in town. When the Great War came he went off with the Navy and never bothered to come back. So Dora and her Mutti went to live with Dora's maternal grandfather in his house on Boston Avenue.

At first the idea of living in that house with the smell of her gruff old Prussian Oma still in it made Dora shaky. But her Opa was delighted to have his little girl back, and also to welcome in Dora, a much more well-behaved child than his own daughter had ever been. Sentimental like all his race, old Mr. Krauss loved having his women around him and as long as they (or at least the conscientious Dora) kept him clean and comfortable he let them go about as they pleased. Dora never got used to this, as her own father had been a conscientious disciplinarian both with her and Mutti. Still wary, she went cautiously, as an empiricist would, devising her theorems, making methodical steps towards uncertain conclusions. She took puffs of the old man's pipe, and he just laughed and patted her. "Don't stunt your growth, Doralein; you don't want to get any littler!"

Though well-formed physically, she'd suffered from a touch

of rheumatism all her life, and perhaps because of this her deportment wasn't the best. She never would carry herself upright, no matter how they scolded or enrolled her in classes at Madam Flowery's School of the Dance (which was where she met Elise). She thumped and slumped around in a way that would have made a bigger girl look clumsy. But Dora was such a slight, transparent thing that her sullen and shambling demeanor made her more endearing, like a kitten with a little limp.

Her eyes were weak, so she wore oval-shaped steel spectacles. Such an elderly contraption on that meek little face made it even sweeter. As she grew old enough to follow her own tastes, she had her hair shingled and dressed herself in unobtrusive frocks of mild green and blue hues that sweetened her sallow complexion. When not at school she rouged her lips, and smoked whenever she got the chance, hoping it would deepen her voice. Elise soon picked up the filthy habit from her, not because it particularly appealed to her, but from a perspective of professional development. To smoke gracefully on the stage was as essential an accomplishment for the Broadway star of her day as swordsmanship is to the classical actor.

*　　*　　*

As far as noise and activity were concerned, Elise's place was a crazyhouse—motors grinding in the garage, kitchen timers going off, cats twining round your legs, brothers and boarders thundering up and down the stairs. For her part, Elise was glad to get out of it and visit Dora. But then the shadows and stillness of Dora's house gave her the creeps. Even when they were children, Dora herself seemed inclined to entertain her on the porch or in the garden. In later years, when Mutti's voice coming from inside the old place seemed to make Dora twitchy and cross, the two girls would go off walking, sometimes taking Turandot, Mutti's little Pekingese, with them.

"I don't know why Mutti got her," Dora complained. "She

hasn't done a thing for her. I raised her myself, I'm the only one who feeds her, the only one who washes her. She'd be one big flea bite if it weren't for me. Mutti said she's been brushing her, but look at this—I'll have to get the scissors and cut out all these mats. And she'll look all stupid and mangy. Poor Turandot!"

Totally undisciplined, Turandot didn't even walk like a normal dog. She'd rustle around like a ballerina on point for a few yards, then flop down under a tree to relax. If you threatened to carry her she'd reluctantly pull herself up and resume a trot, only to stop and spend ten minutes sniffing and biting at some unspeakable delicacy in the grass.

"If it wasn't for Turandot, nobody'd love me," said Dora.

"Everyone loves you, Dora."

Dora nudged Turandot away from the well-gnawed tuft of grass—whatever it was in there, she'd had enough. "No they don't," she said. "And well they shouldn't."

"You mustn't say that. Men are crazy about you. They're always after you."

"Only horrible ones."

Turandot broke into a sudden gallop; they dutifully followed along.

"Oh, they're not ALL horrible," said Elise. "I know for a fact at least two of my brothers think you're adorable."

"But they're so old. And they're all interested in engines and machines. They wouldn't understand me with all my old books and chronic melancholia."

"Well, what sort of man would you want?"

"Depends on who'd have me."

"I imagine we'll both be in big demand when I'm famous and we're rich."

Something must have died among the overgrown grasses just north of the sycamore tree. After sniffing it, Turandot dove cheek-first into it, ecstatically perfuming herself.

"But then my mother says if I go on stage, no decent man will want me," said Elise.

"That can't be true. In this day and age!"

"Mother says the women have changed with the times, but the men haven't."

If there's one thing a young girl can't bear it's the prospect of never being mated, of her youthful blossom withering uncaressed.

"It can't be you can never be married," Dora said quietly. "You're too worthy of love, Elise."

And on impulse, she felt for the slim carnelian ring she'd been wearing, something of her grandmother's that Opa had given her; now she tugged it off, took Elise's hand and wriggled it onto her finger. She'd meant to put it on the middle finger but it went on the other one, the ring finger that was supposed to be reserved for boys. She blushed. So did Elise.

"You can take it off when you're engaged," Dora said shyly.

"I won't, you know."

They walked together in the wake of the scampering dog, laughing a little, too moved to speak.

Chapter 2

High school seemed to increase Dora's nervous irrita-
bility, especially as it separated her all day from Elise (though
they were the same age, Dora was a grade ahead of her friend.)
She cut classes, then stayed home altogether. Again, nothing
happened, as she was past the age when the truant officer would
bother coming after her, and Mutti and Opa (who seldom went
anywhere) always enjoyed her company. Out of boredom with
nothing to do all day, and desperate to get out of the house, she
took a job at Losch's confectionary, and for extra money started
tutoring younger girls in French and German, both subjects at
which she'd excelled in school. "Such industriousness!" said
Opa. He took her to the bank to open a savings account, and
taught her how to balance her passbook. "*This* is what you need
to get on in this world," he told her, clasping her hand around
the little leatherette case.

"But now she'll never have a graduation!" complained Mutti.

No one really worried about what would become of Dora. In
those days women worked, of course—when haven't they?—but
no one actually expected a girl to have such a thing as a career.
And though there was something old-maidish in Dora's habits,
no one looked on her as a potential spinster. There was such a
rare daintiness about her; how could she be left on the shelf?
Naturally some discerning bachelor would stop by Losch's some
day, see her through the glass plucking chocolates or digging ice

cream with a steel scoop as thick as her wrist, point and make his selection: "*That* one."

Unlike Elise, who read all the newest and most shocking novels, Dora preferred history, which has better stories. But she loved and understood the theater, another reason why she was essential to her friend. No one in Elise's family and none of her other acquaintances save Dora really sympathized with her need to go on the stage. Mostly, they thought show business was for gypsies and perverts who weren't wanted in normal society. "At least be a dancer," Elise's mother had said, and tried coaxing her in that direction with satin-ribboned shoes and en point lessons at Madam Flowery's (with poor Dora tottering wincingly alongside her). She had the idea that the Russian ballet was good for young girls, sort of an Eastern Orthodox version of a convent school.

But Elise would be an actress. She would be a real one too, not some amateur theatrical diva or vaudeville soubrette, although as a schoolgirl she tried out for (and generally got a part in) every local play or pageant that she possibly could, laboring in the provinces being an obligatory rite of her professional discipline. But she knew the only real, the only *legitimate* theater on the continent was in New York. If only Broadway shows were like the circus, that picked up wanderlusting locals as they passed through! But Elise and Dora didn't live in a preview town; here they only sent shows whose casts were firmly set. And there was Actor's Equity to conjure with.

Dora and Elise went to every legitimate stage show that came to their city, as often as their pocket books would allow. They always watched in reverent silence, never a crinkle of candy wrapper, never a rustle of program page. At each intermission, Dora would watch Elise gaze longingly into the wings as they reluctantly joined the crush of customers filing out into the lobby. At the curtain call, when moved to do so (which was surprisingly often), Elise would rise to her feet. Dora would, too. And they'd stand and cry "Bravo!" even while others nudged them aside on their way out. Someone on stage must know that someone in this loutish town had noticed, and cared, what beauty had been offered them from the hearts of these questing artists.

Afterwards, Dora would patiently follow her friend around the corner of the theater to the alleyway where the stage door creaked, and loiter there, bundled and umbrellaed as necessary against the wind and the rain. Most of the touring actors just rushed past them towards their rooming houses or the nearest blind pig, but sometimes some of them—often the greatest stars among them—would smile, pause, offer to sign their autograph books, even linger to chat. Though Dora hung back shyly, Elise always had some question or something to say that seemed to startle and please these strange, baroquely dignified creatures of the stage. A few of them ended up walking with the girls all the way to the trolley stop, and one grande dame took them to Losch's for ice cream sodas. These actors were real people, the darlings, if exaggerated ones.

"The minute I graduate, I'm headed for that train to New York," Elise told Dora that night after ice cream with Broadway royalty.

"Why wait?" Dora muttered. She was sort of in the mood to go herself.

"I promised Mother I'd finish school. I've only got three months to go. Anyway, Broadway's full of dummies with pretty faces. I've got to be the smart one."

"You're pretty enough," said Dora kindly.

Elise trotted over to a doorway, leaning in out of the breeze to strike a match for them. "I hate to leave my folks. Not my brothers so much—they're busy with their cars and their love lives. But Mother will be awfully sad when I go."

"Least she cares. Mutti wouldn't mind if I joined the white slave trade."

"Mmm, I'd come along myself for a lark," said Elise, sucking on her Lucky with a grin.

*   *   *

Though ordinarily loath to be seen with her Mutti, Dora some-times went with her on Wednesday and Saturday nights to Spiritualist religious services—or, as the uninitiated might call them, mediumistic seances. Lately Elise had been asking to go too. "*Why?*" snarled Dora. This business of contacting the Other Side wasn't exotic or entertaining to HER.

The services were held in the basement of a residence on the finer end of Boston Avenue owned by a woman medium and her husband, who served the role of a lay minister or compere to the proceedings. They didn't turn off the lights or hold hands round a table, the way they do in movie seances. You sat on folding chairs in rows, as in a normal church, and the service always opened with prayers and some hymns. But after this, things got going in a way that would give an ordinary Christian the heebiejeebies. As a younger child Dora had usually been able to sleep through whatever went on. But as she got older and came to understand what was actually happening there, she stayed awake—she didn't dare do otherwise.

After the soothing opening rituals the lady medium, Mrs. Lelis, sat in a chair on the little platform in front of everyone and went into her trance, withdrawing deep into herself so that other souls would have room to enter her and speak through her lar-ynx. The reverend Mr. Lelis would act as aide and interpreter to these visiting spirits.

Often they didn't just stay inside their hostess, but escaped her body and floated around the platform, playing fitfully with a trumpet or tambourine that lay on the table next to her. Dora never liked it when the spirits got loose. She'd feel the urge to run but force herself to stay still, afraid that if she moved they'd drop their toys and come after her.

Just as scary as the wandering ghosts were the spirit guides who preferred to linger in the vicinity of the medium's voice box. The ones who liked to chat most often were from some tribe of

Indians that used to live on the land before white settlers chased them off, and Dora never trusted their motives for coming back.

At every seance conducted by the Lelises the spirits followed the same protocol, diffidently at first, then with increasing passion. The first ghost to take control of Mrs. Lelis's vocal cords was always a weak one who made sounds that were indistinct, far away-sounding. Then suddenly some dead Indian brave would push through with loud, gruff barks and shouts that made you jump. Dora envisioned them as very wild, fierce Indians with long hair and buckskins. Their raw, violent howls and mutterings made her heart pound, tears of fright fill her eyes.

Conjured up by these savage yammerings, the gentle Christian dead would come and call out to the loved ones who'd come to visit them. And the bereaved, hearing their dear voices, would groan and sob, and tears would spatter like rain from their faces.

After a whispered exchange with his entranced wife, Mr. Lelis might say, "There's a mother here, she has blonde hair, she hasn't been dead very long," and someone would cry for their mother, and then the mother's voice would answer back, telling her shuddering child that she was happy now, the pain was gone, and not to mourn so much. This was the main reason the dead came back, to break the cruel illusion of death and reassure those who hadn't passed through its veils yet that those who had gone on to the other side suffered nothing, still loved them, for all intents and purposes were still with them.

"That medium must be good, to do all those voices," Elise said.

But that was the thing, according to Dora. What was fake here, and how could you tell? While you sat among these goings-on you'd have to be something less than human not to feel the joy and relief and awesome fear vibrating in every living molecule around you. But after, in your own ordinary territory, you'd start questioning what you'd felt at the Lelises'. Are the spirits really with us? Are there disembodied human awarenesses concentrating on the lives of the living, watching us all the time?

Isn't that a terrifying idea? Reassuring too, though, the way you felt playing on your own street, where the mothers and grandmothers watched you from their windows, knowing what might happen to you, ready to make sure it never happened.

"So all those people go just to talk to their dead relatives," said Elise. "Well, I suppose really famous dead people wouldn't bother to come even if you did call them, just like here in the real world. Who does your mother talk to? Your granny?"

"Oma? No, never when I was there," said Dora. "I can't imagine she'd want to."

"Who, then? How many dead people does she know?"

"Nobody she ever talks about. But people don't always go there to talk to anyone in particular. Sometimes they just have a question, or they need some advice, and when it comes to that any spirit can help you."

"Really?"

"Sure, you can ask them anything, they'll tell you."

"That's creepy. So dead people know everything?"

"Well, they look it up. There's a book in the spirit world where everything that ever happens is written down, called the Akashik Records. So if you ask a question, the spirits know where to find the answer."

"They can look it up, like your Uncle Ted."

"Uncle Ted's gonna be great with the Akashik Records. When he passes on, I'll go to him for everything I want to know."

"Have you ever asked the spirits anything?"

"Never!"

"Has your mother ever asked?"

"No, she just goes to listen. I think she's waiting for something to happen. Somebody to show up and ask for her."

"Who do you think she's waiting for?"

"My father."

"He's not dead, is he?"

"Don't think so."

"Don't you have to be dead to be in a seance?"

"Well, usually you are, but I don't see why you'd have to be. Everybody's got a spirit, and anybody can leave their bodies whenever they want to. We just don't think to do it most of the time. But it can happen if you're asleep or if you're in a trance, you can float right out of yourself. My mother said one night she was lying down listening to the radio, and she realized all of a sudden she was looking down at herself. Said it scared the hell out of her. She won't let me play music when she's in the house anymore."

"Your mother's nuts."

"You don't say!" sneered Dora. "When did you notice?"

*　　*　　*

The day of Elise's graduation Dora had said she was sick and couldn't go, not even to the celebration dinner at Elise's house afterwards. She spent the day up in the attic reading *Eminent Victorians* and gnawing an old stick of horehound candy she'd found in a corner, just like her childhood all over again.

She was too devastated even to make the effort to deliver Elise's graduation present. It was a necklace she'd fashioned herself out of an old lavaliere of her grandmother's and a pearl she'd abstracted from the string her mother had given her some months before to get mended at the jeweler's. It would be better to get started now on what it would be like when Elise was gone, than wait till it was actually happening. Holding the pearl lavaliere back was a way to have something of her, even before she was gone. Besides, it made her hate herself more, which felt better, in some way or other.

As it was nearly summer, it took longer for night to come, but Dora patiently waited for it to be too dark to read, so she'd have nothing to look at but the dark until the moon came up. Elise, however, found her despite the cobwebs and gloom. She actually had lugged her luggage all the way out to Dora's garage and hid it there the night before; she'd planned it that way, she said, so Dora could drive her to the station.

"Why didn't you tell me?" asked Dora.

"Because . . . well, you're just not an actress, that's all," Elise said gently. "If you knew, even if you never said anything, they'd look at you and figure it all out. And if I had to say goodbye to Mother—I couldn't bear it. So I'm sneaking out like a thief in the night."

Dora started to cry. She wanted to go with her so much. But Elise said it would be better for her to stay behind for now. "It can be pretty rough when you're just starting out in New York. You've got to starve and sleep with bedbugs and who knows what else. That's not for you, Dora. I know you're miserable here, but it won't be much longer, I promise. Don't cry."

"Not crying," said Dora, wondering how she could see her tears in the dark.

"I'll send for you as soon as I'm making enough money to take care of the both of us. You'll never have to work at stupid jobs like Losch's, because you'll have a job: you'll be my companion. I'll introduce you to all the best people, all the best men. We'll marry you off into the Social Registah."

"I don't want to be married," Dora sobbed.

"Then you'll stay with me. We'll have a Boston marriage, and have Pekingeses instead of children and wear rings that match."

"Oh!" cried Dora, and pounded out of the room.

"Now, what did I say," wondered Elise, but then her friend stumbled back with the old velvet box, with the pearl lavaliere inside it. Now it was Elise's turn to drop tears on the attic floor.

"You are my dearest, dearest girl," she whispered wetly, "and I'm going to work so hard, it won't be long—"

"I know!"

"Let's go, let's get it over with!"

Elise could never operate Flivvy, no matter how many times Dora had tried to teach her. She marveled at how well Dora could maneuver and manipulate the little knobby things all over the

dashboard and floor, how the heavy, grimy monster sprang obediently to her touch. Fragile as Dora seemed, there was a certain
tensile resilience to her. She'd make a fine New Yorker. And I'll
see to it that she gets the life she deserves, Elise told herself. Get
her away from that crazy mother of hers. German mothers and no
fathers, that's the curse of us both.

There wasn't a porter in sight. They lugged Elise's baggage to
the platform, then sat hand in hand, waiting. A drunk had wandered onto the track out near Chicago, giving them three extra
hours together.

"I don't know how I'll live, with you gone," said Dora.

"Just keep breathing," said Elise. "Soon we'll be together
forever."

Chapter 3

Dora's Opa had more or less disowned Dora's Uncle Ted, and Mutti wasn't speaking to him either, so Dora saw him mostly when she stopped by the library where he worked. Dora went more often now Elise was gone. It was one of her favorite places in the world, and these days the only place she ever felt really happy anymore.

Everyone knew her there, and better yet, left her alone. They let her go down the back stairways to the closed stacks, where only people who worked there were ordinarily allowed to go. This was the part she really loved—the dark rows of bookshelves running the length of enormous rooms, floor to ceiling, mostly dead quiet, sometimes echoing with sounds of a library page moving through the stacks to snatch a book somebody'd ordered out front. Some of the pages wore roller skates; you'd hear them clumping down the stairs and crackling through the aisles.

Uncle Ted worked in the basement of the library in a big room with no window, only walls and walls of books, unmarked with library labels, most of them very dusty. Uncle Ted called them "the backlog." For each of these books, Uncle Ted made up the little cards that went in the catalog drawers upstairs. He worked slowly and intensely, rattling two-fingered at his ash-spattered typewriter, puffing at his cigarette, scowling or snickering to himself. Dora would spend hours in this realm of Uncle Ted's, reading, making pencil sketches on old discarded catalog cards, prowling the stacks. She loved it, it was peaceful as the grave, except for the typewriter and the whoosh of skates.

Usually Dora liked to spend her time in the darker corners of the closed stacks, browsing for old rare volumes detailing Flemish court intrigues or the secrets of the great alchemists of Prague. But lately one set of shelves more regularly drew her interest. They were restricted shelves, for use by scholars and doctors only, and were kept in an area apart from the unforbidden books. Not even the pages were allowed to touch them, only librarians, like Uncle Ted. Dora didn't dare linger there even to read the spines; she'd spot what she wanted in the catalog beforehand, go grab it, and dash. She'd look it over later, in Uncle Ted's office.

Uncle Ted was sanguine about Dora's reading habits. He said there wasn't a thing in his library that wasn't fit for an intelligent girl to examine. He was a freethinker and it was largely due to his determined advocacy that Dora's secret book nook existed at all. "People love to burn books," he told her. "Especially if they haven't read them."

"Why? They're just books. They can't hurt anybody."

"Not unless that's what they're looking for," said Uncle Ted.

*   *   *

Mutti was just intolerable now, whining and worse, wanting to *talk* all the time. Once again she was getting into Opa's precious cache of Oma's homemade blackberry wine. Opa scolded her but didn't have the heart to do anything about it. Anyway, Mutti always managed to find where he hid the bottles. "Ladies your mother's age can get very sad, Dora," Opa told her. "Sometimes a little something can help them."

With Mutti getting plastered and passing out on Dora's bed half the time (she never did get used to sleeping by herself and Turandot wouldn't have anything to do with her at night as she made such terrible snoring noises), Dora felt less at home than ever before. She was getting too old to hide in the attic—it was starting to make her feel like the first Mrs. Rochester. Her hours at Losch's weren't that long, which was just as well, as the other girls were so catty and idiotic she couldn't stand it. She still had her refuge under the library with Uncle Ted, but not on Sundays, and not at night, when Mutti was at her worst.

Now that Elise was in New York and was only available to her through letters, Dora felt terribly anxious, stranded within her lonely self. When the buzz of her blood got too loud to bear she would take Flivvy out of the city, beyond the straggling townships and farms until she was nowhere. She would sit on the fender, facing a flat horizon surrounded by stumps of slain pine and sycamore that the lumbermen had plundered, watching the light disappear, not daring or caring to look at the gas gauge to see if she had enough to go back. Poor Dora, what will become of me? Don't know, Dora.

As soon as Dora got Elise's first letter, with her first address in New York on the back of the envelope, she wrote back immediately, long long letters, sometimes two or three a day. As for Elise, well, composition was never her strongest subject, and perhaps predictably she was no great letter writer. Her notes and postcards were affectionate and bright, hysterically funny sometimes, but irregular in coming, and frustratingly lacking in detail. But she said she loved Dora's letters, so Dora kept writing to her regularly; it helped.

Occasionally Dora would get letters back, return to sender, from some landlady who couldn't be bothered with forwarding it to Elise's latest address. It hardly mattered. Elise always had news to report, some audition, somebody she'd met who might help her, some wonderful show she'd seen. While for all her rambling verbosity Dora really had only one letter to write: I'm here still, so is everyone else, nothing has changed.

Sometimes Dora felt so weird she wondered if she was crazy. Especially when she was downtown, working or taking a walk, she'd seem to feel a slight separation between herself and her fleshly container, conscious that she was riding around inside the body of a girl with a name and attributes that she, the inner Dora, didn't necessarily share. It slowed her down, watching herself as though crouched on her own brain, observing her bodily movements slowing down self-consciously as she, not-she, wondered whether she might at the next moment freeze up like a switched-off machine and never move again. Usually she just kept on going. And no one seemed to notice anything wrong with her.

One time at the trolley stop a young man did strike up a conversation with her, possibly sensing her tilted state, maybe taking advantage of her defenselessness, maybe hoping to help. "You can sit down here," he told her.

Dora had been hovering, not sure if she wanted to take the empty half of the bench next to him, not even sure that waiting for the trolley would be good for her at this point. Walking sometimes jolted her soul and body back into alignment, working off some of her panic and at least getting her closer to home. She needed to make up her mind; she felt cross at this man who had no right to interrupt her crisis.

"You look a little faint," said the young blond man.

"I'm not!" said Dora. "I've never fainted in my life."

"You just look peaked. Come on, sit."

He got up, sidling aside so that Dora could sit in the middle of the bench, and not worry about having to be next to a strange man. Which was what he should have done before, Dora realized, but she automatically thanked him anyway.

"Maybe you're cold," he said, "it's getting chilly."

"The sun's not out," said Dora. She didn't bother to think of anything interesting to say. He was polished, dimpled, vaguely insincere-seeming in his little black Harold Lloyd spectacles.

"Gloomy day."

"I like the clouds," Dora said defensively. "I like a gray sky. Makes me feel protected."

"Oh. Do you get freckles in the sun?"

The fresh horror of being trapped with this bland person made

Dora forget her fears of depersonalization. "I'm not afraid of freckles," she said.

"I am. Make me look even more like a little kid than I already do."

But if you didn't want to look like a kid, you'd try to straighten those curls out, Dora thought. And try not to chirrup so much.

"I'm Stokes Chesney," said the young blond man. "And who are you?"

Dora was so frankly offended by his tone of voice, as though he'd said "Who are you LITTLE GIRL???" that she really wasn't going to say anything. But then he said, "I know your name is Dora because I've heard the other girls call you. At Losch's. I have an awful sweet tooth, I go there a lot. You probably never noticed me."

"I never notice anybody," said Dora. That wasn't true. She had seen him at Losch's, several times recently, and had avoided him. She always let the other girls wait on the ones who wanted to chat.

"Are you hungry?" asked this Chestnut person. "I am, I haven't had anything all day."

"Not really hungry."

"Well, maybe a Coke or a malted milk, then? My treat. I suppose you don't want to go to Losch's."

"I don't mind."

"It's right up the street. Which must be why you're here. Aren't I brilliant."

Dora went along with him. She really didn't care. She let him order for her, didn't touch it. He didn't seem to notice. He thought he was going to cheer her up, she supposed.

Apparently Chestnut was some sort of divinity student who didn't live out here normally, but had been serving as an apprentice pastor at a church belonging to whatever denomination he was. Now he was preparing for a journey to Transylvania in Europe, where he was going to study and confer with the

Transylvanian scholars of his religion. "The question to decide is, do we believe in God?" said Chestnut boy.

"You should have thought of that before you went to the seminary!"

"Oh, you can be a Unitarian and never make up your mind. But it helps if you've thought through all the possibilities. Especially if you're leading a church, you have to know things like which hymnal to use, do you use the wedding service that mentions God or the newer one? And people come to you for advice. You have to know something about what they're going to ask you first. You can't just make it up as you go along, like some of those Christians do."

"You're not a Christian, then?"

"Some of us are. My father is. But he's a capitalist too. They go hand in hand, you know. I'm sorry, are you Christian?"

"I don't know what I am. I guess I'm a Theosophist."

"Theosophy's interesting. Kind of out of date where I come from. But then we got started with the table-rappings and such a long time before it caught on out here. I'm from the East."

"I know some people named Chestnut," said Dora, with a sudden swell of affability.

"Ches-_ney_," Stokes murmured gently.

He did smell very good, like sandalwood and well-tended old books. Dora imagined his faith was one that involved kneeling on straw mats and striking gongs.

"I'd love to come to your church sometime," said Stokes.

"I'd like to see yours too."

"Would you?"

It was just around the corner. He took her inside. It was just like a real church, gray faux-medieval stone, colored windows, big wooden monks' benches for the congregation to sit on. But there was no altar, just a podium in front, and no crosses or candles. It seemed unusually bright inside, as though no spirits lurked there.

"Back home we just have a little clapboard meeting house," said Stokes. "This seems a bit much to me."

"Seems like something missing here," said Dora. "I guess it's Jesus."

"Poor Jesus! No, I never liked the way they have him hanging up naked and strangling. Is that the way to remember the Prince of Peace, as a bleeding wreck?"

"So you . . . acknowledge Jesus?"

"Sure, I like him a lot," said Stokes. "Don't always agree with him." His softened vowels, the slight bleat of his "a"s, did sound Eastern.

They ran across a janitor who greeted Stokes happily, and the minister's wife and her friend—dressed in Indian beads and batiks, like something you might find studying ceramics at the Art Institute—who accosted Stokes with great warmth and repeatedly told him how much they were going to miss him when he went to Transylvania. So cheery and glib as he was, at least he wasn't a fake. Standing there listening to them go on and on, Dora started to feel almost as though she were going to miss him herself.

By the time he walked her home she was exhausted, but felt much better.

"Not to be forward or anything," said Stokes, "but would you like a postcard from Transylvania?"

"Certainly."

"All right then," said Stokes, taking out a pad and pencil. "So you live at 23 Boston Avenue . . . and, excuse me, here I've been calling you Dora all day. I really should say Miss Krauss, shouldn't I?"

"Krauss is my grandfather's name," said Dora.

"Oh, you have a different name than his?"

"My father's. . . . Doesn't matter. I'm thinking of changing it back."

"If you don't like your name you could always marry out of it."

Dora sort of snorted, then wished she hadn't, but Stokes didn't seem to notice; he was busy making notations.

"Well, I'd better go in," said Dora. "Have a good time in Transylvania."

"I'll do my best. Au 'voir, Dora."

The first thing she thought of when she was alone again, climbing the stairs to her room as quietly as possible in hopes Mutti wouldn't catch her and corner her with some dreadful soliloquy, was telling Elise all about Stokes Chesney, as she always did whenever she had a new man story. But should she bother, would it mean anything to Elise now, considering the adventures she was having now, many probably in the company of real New York men?

Elise was on the stage now, really and absolutely. She'd even had a speaking part in her last play, which closed out of town, but that had certainly not been Elise's fault (a clipping she sent Dora referred to Elise as a "bug-eyed Bea Lillie," which Elise assured her was good) and her director had recommended her for an even better part with even more lines. There was also a possibility that she might test for the movies, though Elise spoke of this with some contempt.

In other words, Elise was making good, and the summons for Dora to join her might come at any time now. Glad as she was at the idea, proud as she was of her dear friend's generosity and valor and ingenuity, Dora didn't have the heart to confess to her that now, as things had turned out, she couldn't possibly accept Elise's offer of lifelong luxury and companionship. Though it wrung her heart to admit it, she couldn't do such a thing to her dearest Elise, to inflict herself on this wonderful girl who was just beginning a dazzling life, just at the point when she, Dora, was drawing to a slow and painful close as a psychological entity and, she feared, a biological one as well.

The truth was there wasn't much left of Dora anymore. She had lost weight and had pains inside she didn't even want to guess at. Her crazy, shameful feelings of fright and unreality grew worse every second. She couldn't make the daily trip down the street to Losch's anymore without agonies of panic and hesitation. Even at home, she'd have seizures of terror, for no reason at all. The very idea of boarding a train to New York City, let alone attempting to live there, frankly terrified her. She felt sick constantly, her muscles and veins burning as though filled with poison. The spirit crouching on her brain, riding her suffering body around, wasn't taking any of this seriously, as if it were already ready to fly the coop.

She felt sorry for poor Opa, who if anything happened to her would be left alone with Mutti, but even more for her Turandot; if not for Dora, who would brush out her tangles, make sure she had her daily milk? The little dog sensed that something was wrong, and clung to her all day, watching her warily. The animal saw her sick aura, smelt it perhaps, as the humans around her could not.

Chapter 4

It got darker and grayer. A few days before Christmas there was a little snow that stuck to the grass and reflected the fading sunlight, but it melted by the next morning. Dreading the daily journey home in the dark, Dora quit Losch's. "Too bad," said Mutti, "at least you met people there."

Still needing to get out of the house, starved for light perhaps, Dora tried going to the movies. It was New Year's Eve; she hadn't been to a picture in months, she realized. In fact, she hadn't been near any sort of theater since Elise left.

It was a mistake to go. She hadn't looked at what was on, she'd just picked the theater with the biggest screen and the prettiest decorations. It was, in fact, the Odeon, where Elise had seen Max Linder all those years ago. But this was no comedy, in fact, it was the worst possible show that poor Dora could have stumbled into. It was one of those miserable creepy movies about unhappy clowns. Why did they keep making these wretched hideosities? They hadn't even had the decency to advertise it truthfully—there was no clown or circus in the title or on the posters—and Lon Chaney, the king of miserable clown movies, wasn't the star so she couldn't have guessed. The featured actor was in fact Hermann Prinz, the brilliant German tragedian, whose stunning, baroquely chiseled and curlicued face was the last you'd dream they'd put the hideous clown-white over. What a waste of his beauty!

It was a damn dark German-style movie, historical melodrama.

Hermann was a disinherited nobleman forced to make his living clowning for stinking low crowds, while the beautiful princess who loved him believed he had died, and was letting herself be sold in marriage to a leering degenerate with pointy chin, nose and eyebrows. Dora cried, but it wasn't the good kind of crying, the deep sobs and gushes that clear out your sinuses and refresh your brain and blood with oxygen. This torturous anxiety of hers, fortified by the revolting carnival of pain onscreen, brought on the worst kind of weeping: the hard, quiet grimace, eyes swollen nearly shut, tears that stung all the way down to stain your blouse with mascara and powder that would never come off.

The clown Hermann's torments were so cruel she couldn't stand it, even watching was like participating in his torture, or at least standing by and letting it happen to him. She knew there had to be a comforting resolution to the story—some reunion with his noble girl friend most probably, as she wasn't the sort of star that got killed off—but how could it be happy, what happiness would ever make life tolerable for Hermann and his love, who'd have to live every day with the foul, humiliating memories of what they'd suffered? The very idea of a happy ending became so false to Dora she refused to stay for it, though she knew the dramatic resolution must, by its sacred ritual function, purge her of at least some terror and pity. But she was already drained to the point of pain, dry as a bone from lost moisture, her cheeks crusted with salt. Now, as she fled the temple of clown-agony, her lips cracked and smarted in the freezing wind that smacked big fat icy scales of snow into her cheeks and eyes; her stockings got soaked and her feet froze in her thin-soled shoes, and she stumbled four or five times on her way to the trolley.

One thing that would make her feel better would be to write to Elise. She'd do it when she got home. But when she'd made it home and looked through the mail—the last delivery of the year, as it was New Year's Eve—she recognized a letter she'd sent Elise not long ago—her birthday letter, in fact, in which Dora had folded a bit of lace she'd crocheted for her, and a rather silly poem she'd written called "On Turning Eighteen."

On the envelope, scrawled rudely over the neatly printed address, were the words NOT AT. This had been the last address Elise had given Dora. So Elise hadn't gotten her birthday greeting. Had she gotten her Christmas letter, either? Was she sitting alone tonight, wondering why Dora had forgotten her? Exhausted and parched as she was, Dora banged her fists against the stair-rails and sobbed.

It didn't occur to Dora that there were other ways to contact Elise: writing to her care of her theatrical agency, for instance, or asking her mother if she had her new address. Weariness, and anticipation of the isolation that the impending holiday would impose on her, overcame her reason. The New Year crawled nearer, stopping everything dead. Tomorrow was New Year's Day, of course, and the day after that was Sunday. The snow itself was closing in thickly, smothering the world outside. Turandot kept close to her, curving up against her with a protective sweep of her feathery tail, not wanting to lose her.

Dora's throat hurt, but she never thought to drink water. She went up to bed, but the absurdity of sleeping struck her and she got up abruptly.

*   *   *

In fine weather, before the terrors had overtaken her, Dora had taken comfort in driving Flivvy out to the ravaged wilderness outside the city, escaping the damned old house and her mother's stinks and snores and Opa's pathetic putterings. But there was no getting out tonight. New Year's Eve, and no parties to go to, no crowds to disappear into; everyone was home, locked up as she was. There was a blizzard going on.

It was two feet deep at the lowest, with the wind sifting the hard, bright particles into drifts as high as the downstairs roof, from what she could see from her window. The garage door was right against the wind; it would be sealed with ice, and the frozen snow banks would be far too hard to ever dig out, with the gales shoving back the snow as soon as you'd shoveled it. The automobile itself would just sit and spin its wheels, even if you could get it out on the road. But there was still a means of escape, still somewhere Flivvy could take her tonight.

The wind scoured her face, plastered her flannel gown with crusts of ice. You couldn't see more than a few yards in front of you. Dora just guessed where the garage would be. It hurt so much to dig her legs into that snow she almost wished she'd worn shoes.

She'd expected to have to scrabble her way through the drifts in order to open the little side door to the garage, but it was easy to find and open. Someone'd already been there earlier to clear away the drift, it seemed, though all traces of footsteps and mitten-prints had been blasted away. It was a little more trouble getting the door closed securely, but she pushed hard and did it.

Billions of tiny ice antimacassars hurled themselves at the windows as she did her wincing toe-dance across the searingly cold paved floor, less exhausting to cross than the snow but just as painful. Suicidal crystals would plaster themselves against the doors, sealing all the cracks she'd made going in, piling in lemming-lumps on roadbeds, making them impassible with their soft bodies; no doctor or fireman could make it through them, and there would be no urgency anyway, in ten or twenty minutes. That's all it would take, from what she'd heard. Turn the key, lie still and breathe deep. Flivvy was fast and strong and would take her away past roads and everything.

The car windows were all frozen up. You couldn't see in to where she was going to put herself. So she gasped when she pried the little black door panel open and saw the shadowy heap on the back seat. Someone had beaten her to it!

But the motor wasn't on . . . she didn't smell anything. There was no key in the ignition—well, of course, she had that in her hand. Who was it? Her first thought was Mutti. But it couldn't be;

she'd heard Mutti well enough, up in her room flopped on the chaise longue, making noises like two infirm coloraturas moving furniture.

It was Elise's coat, the pretty, soft burgundy wool Dora herself had helped Elise pick out at Elise's favorite fabric store. She'd sat with Elise, watching her work it with shears and sewing machine treadle into a mantle fit for a Broadway star. Now tossed like a lumpy blanket over the rigid little body on the black back seat.

Dora's dazed, half-frozen brain saw the sense in this. Of course Elise was here, she'd gone on ahead of her, and was waiting for Dora to join her. So gamely Dora slid down onto the icy leather and under the soft satin-lined coat, slipping one arm round the cold, hard waist, the other under the neck. She could feel her heart pumping the warmth from her breast into the vast, absorbing chill of Elise's spine. She held the tears back in her eyes, waiting for them to freeze.

Like the voice of M. Valdemar, it came not from the unmoving lips, but hollowly from the back of Elise's tongue. Dora thought at first maybe it was a seat spring underneath the leather, making that soft croaking noise. But it was Elise's voice; she heard it, felt her voice box thrumming against her fingers:

"'s it midnight yet?"

Chapter 5

It took both of them shoving at the door to get back out, it was snowing that hard. Elise made Dora put on her own coat and galoshes. She couldn't believe Dora had gone out into this white hell in just her nightie. "You could catch your death! Are you nuts?"

They were both madly cold, so they sat in front of the stove. As she rubbed Dora's poor little ice-cubed toes back to life again, Elise remarked that Dora had probably saved her life. "I didn't know the snow had gotten that deep. I could've been trapped out there with no heat or food or anything. How did you know to come wake me? The spirits must've told you. How did you get out there? Were you sleepwalking? Your poor toes must be frost-bit!"

"No, they can't be," Dora murmured. "They'd be black, not red."

The garage hadn't been Elise's first choice of where to spend the night. Seeing that all the lights were out, Elise had assumed that Dora's family were either at a party or had decided to make an early night of it, and she hated to disturb them. She'd decided to shelter in Flivvy till morning, then figure out what to do next. She'd spent her last nickel on carfare to get to Dora's house, which ruled out a hotel or even a flophouse. And she couldn't go to her own house—that was for sure. "My FATHER's there," she snapped.

Once she'd arrived at the station, Elise had gone home expecting to crawl into bed with Mother as in the old days. But Mother wasn't alone. Elise had come upon her in bed with her own father—Elise's father, that is. Now that all the children were gone, the two had reconciled, and were now enjoying an illicit evening before their planned remarriage. "So I can't go home," Elise scowled.

"Stay here with me," Dora begged.

"I really don't know where else to go. I barely slept on that damn train."

"Are you hungry?"

"Oh, Dora . . . I could eat *you*."

Measure out the coffee beans; turn the handle of the grinder; fill the water up to there; set the grounds up in their metal pedestal; turn up the gas flame. The tasks are there, as long as we live, to lead us calmly back into the routine of life.

"But why are you back?" said Dora, suddenly thinking of it. "I thought you had a show!"

"Not anymore," Elise said, munching her liverwurst.

"What happened?"

Elise finished the last bite of her sandwich—except for the crusts, she never ate those—and went to get more coffee.

"How can I tell you? I don't know if I can," she said. "I did something so stupid. . . . "

Dora didn't want to hear. But she felt Elise needed her to. Weakly she whispered: "Was it a man?"

"There was a man. What he did to me. . . . Oh god, I can't tell you."

Dora grabbed her knuckles in her teeth and squeezed her eyes shut. Her heart had just broken, and now she would die.

"Oh, Dora. Oh, my goodness gracious."

Elise held Dora in her lap, stroking her pale, damp hair while the poor girl cried as hard as she might have hours ago if she hadn't walked out of that Hermann Prinz film, but stayed in the cinema-temple to receive the catharsis she'd needed so badly.

When Dora had quieted down, Elise got up, took Dora's shoulder in one hand, a glass of milk in the other, and led her quietly as she could up to her bed. Burrowing in beside her, kicking her toes defiantly into the ice-cold sheets to warm the both of them, she tried as best she could to explain.

*　　*　　*

"He was a friend of my director's, he'd been to one of our rehearsals and wanted to meet me. I'd heard of him before, he was working on a picture at Astoria Studios—not a big one, but he was on his way up, everybody said so. I thought he must be one of these little Jews from Vienna, wanting to get to Hollywood and earn his 'Von.' But he wasn't like that at all. He had blue eyes, for one thing. He told me, you're going to be the most original, thrilling actress of your generation. I said yes, and he said, would you like to make a test with me, I've got a picture I'm going to pitch, and if I can capture what I see in you on film, that will sell my project.

"Well, I talked to my director, and I talked to the people I know at Astoria, and everyone said he's going to be very big, you must do it. I said, I don't want to go into pictures. They said, if it was good enough for Bernhardt it's good enough for you, and if you get tired of the money in Hollywood you can always come back to New York. So I told him I'd do it.

"I came to the studio the night before we left for New Haven. I had to wait until they finished the last set-up for the film he was working on; they were going to let us shoot it there when they were through. He brought in his own camera. It was a little hand-cranked one that he'd bought in Germany after the war; he said it was still the best one he'd ever worked with. He wanted me to play a scene with a dead kitten, but I just couldn't do it with the real one he'd brought. So he took off his socks, and he stuffed one inside of the other, and I played it with that, hiding it in my hands so you couldn't tell. He said it didn't show in the shot anyway.

"We were still at it when the regular crew came in to set up the next morning. He was brilliant, but what a slave driver! He just talked and talked and talked at me, put that eyebrow up here, put that eyebrow down there, look up at that lamp like it was your long-lost mother, he wouldn't let up on me one minute! I never worked so hard for anyone before, I never gave so much. And there was no script, no one to play off of: just him, him, HIM and his voice and his commands, running me ragged. I was so tired, I'd lost count of how many times I'd done the scene, and stopped noticing when the camera was running. I felt empty, I'd used up every emotion just to please this crazy man, and was it worth it? I'd missed the train to New Haven. I was practically dead, but I had to run home to get my grip and makeup box, and then run for the next train, to catch up with my company. I felt I'd let them down, and I wasn't even sure it had been worth it for me to make that test. I tried to remember what I'd done and it was like a dream I'd forgotten while I was waking from it.

"I got to New Haven, I found the hotel, I got a few hours' sleep, and I thought I was going to be all right. No one was angry at me, they knew me, they knew I'd be there in time for the opening. I got to the theater with plenty of time to spare. I hate to rush. I always like to relax, do my breathing exercises, check my costumes and props—I hate last-minute emergencies, and everyone's in such a tizzy when you're out of town. It's just better to be calm, you know?

"My part in that show was very important. My director said this girl was even more important than the ingenue, she was the spark that made the whole piece go, and that's why I had to play her. Because I had the FIRE.

"Well, I didn't feel firey in New Haven. But I was there for opening night. And everything was fine, everything went just as it should. I did everything just as we'd rehearsed it, I was on my marks, I said my lines the right way. But my voice sounded funny to me, kind of private and muffled, like it sounds when you're wearing a mask. I felt hot, the lights seemed too bright. And then I had a strange feeling, as though I was watching myself, from outside myself. I thought, will I remember the next line? And I did, I went on with the scene just like I'd learned it. But there was something wrong. I started to breathe harder, I looked at the other actors to see if they could notice a change, and I think they did. I think the audience did too, they were awfully quiet.

"The show went on. I didn't miss a cue. I got through what I had to do, I don't know how, I felt so empty, so ashamed. I ran out right after the curtain, and ran away from anyone who tried to talk to me, and ran back to the hotel and locked myself in.

"My director was so sweet. He made me come out, he took me to his room and made love to me, and then he made me eat a steak and gave me champagne and ice cream. He said all I'd had was just a little stage fright. But it wasn't that. Something was really wrong, Dora. Something was missing from me. Whatever it was that made me what I was and wanted to be, that sent me up on that stage to begin with, had just gone and left me up there, just a little scared dummy who had no business being in front of an audience, didn't want to be there, didn't have any idea how she'd gotten there.

"I was mortified. They wouldn't let me see the papers, I knew the notices had to be awful, but they said they wouldn't do the show without me, I had to go on. And I did, it was awful. The backers pulled out before the second act even started. I killed that show with my bare hands! I said, God, forgive me, I didn't mean to do this to you! All we did was cry all the way back to New York. We loved that show so much!

"They gave us our money. I just went home and packed up everything and paid off the landlady. Then I went back to the station and got back on the train I'd come in on last June. It was that or jump in front of it."

Elise took a final sip of milk, then let Turandot lap the rest from the rim of the glass.

"But I couldn't do that," she said. "Because you were waiting for me. And I could do anything to myself, but I couldn't do it to you."

"Oh, *me*, what do *I* matter? Poor Elise!"

"What kills me is, I love it there so much. You talk there, and people understand you. So many girls there are just like you. You're a type, do you realize it? I'M a type. Out here we're freaks, but back there we're really sort of ordinary. You'd be going to lectures and galleries, and I'd be sprawled out on Persian pillows smoking a hookah or something, and nobody'd look twice."

"Sounds wonderful."

"There are trees there, Dora. They're not all chopped down. Not in the city, I mean outside, in the mountains, along the river. It's pretty countryside, you can see why all the rich Dutchmen bought it up."

"I never think of there being anything in New York but New York."

"Oh, there's a whole state. And New Jersey and Connecticut, too. All full of people like you, Dora. People with culture and brains. Well, in New York, anyway."

"We can go back again. Whenever you're ready."

Elise made a weary sound.

"I know something's wrong," said Dora. "I know I can't possibly know what's happening to you. But I won't let you suffer alone."

She smiled, feeling so brave and loving it. She nestled close to her friend, and squeezed her tight.

"I know you came back like a little hurt animal crawling home to die," she whispered. "But you know what, you're going to live. Because you've got to do what God and Shakespeare and Sherwood Anderson need you to do, and no amount of discouragement in the world must ever stop you.

"But don't think about that now. Just rest. And when you're ready to travel again, we'll go. We'll get my money out of the bank and get on the train and go where the stages are, because that's where you've got to be. I don't need looking after, really. I can work, I can sweep floors and shovel butterfat. Somebody's got to take care of *you*, Elise. And that's me, I guess."

Chapter 6

The exhausted girls slept straight through New Year's Day, until it was night again and Mutti, still purple under the eyes from last night's infusion of fermented blackberry, came to call them for dinner. "I wish I'd known you were visiting last night," she told Elise, "I would have stayed up with you girls!"

After the dishes were cleared Mutti excused herself—she did look nearly ready to faint—and Opa went out to shovel the sidewalks again. "He's going to kill himself," said Dora fretfully.

"Oh, that's what men love to do," said Elise. "Let's make him a nice stollen."

Dora watched as Elise measured out the ingredients, swiftly kneaded out the sweetened dough, unfolded a clean dishcloth to cover it as it rose. There was nothing about this solid, bright-eyed girl that seemed the least bit morbid or depressed. Whatever it was that Elise felt she was missing, Dora couldn't see it. She was Elise, as ever a pleasure to see.

"Is your mother going to her seance tonight?" Elise asked.

"No, she's down for the count."

"Are they having it, though?"

"Oh yes, every Saturday, even holidays."

"I thought maybe they'd be canceled with the snow."

"The Lelises never cancel if anyone shows up."

"Will you take me?"

They bound themselves up in scarves and shawls, though

this night wasn't as miserable as last. The snowing was over, and
with the wind stilled the cold didn't hurt anymore. They kept to
the swept and shoveled walkways, and stepped in the tracks left
by the sledding kids. It was a pretty, bright evening under the
stars and streetlamps, and Dora would have been happy just
walking, but Elise kept her marching quickly in the intended
direction, wanting to get there on time, which they were. They'd
just stamped the snow out of their treads when they heard the
music start downstairs.

*   *   *

Elise seemed to take to this haunt of crazy women, with its faint
smell of must, dead mice and patchouli, its gramophone recital
of "In the Garden" sung by a nanny goat with organ-grinder
accompaniment. She sat as though she was in a real church,
hands gravely folded, watching and concentrating hard as Mrs.
Lelis nodded as in sleep, lowering her eyes in greeting as the
spirits entered her.

Dora felt Elise's little fingers squeeze hers when Tucum the
Tonquish brave barked his greeting; she shuddered herself when
he began his keening necromantic incantation. Thank God there
didn't appear to be bereaved children among the worshippers
tonight. She felt so nervous, she would have cried herself into a
faint, had the mothers come.

Then she heard Elise's voice, deep, rich, and ringing beside
her: "*Where is it?*"

Dora turned and stared, wanting to shush her, not daring to.
What was she doing? You weren't supposed to yell out in the
middle of services, you waited till you were called upon. Now the
spirits would be mad.

Mrs. Lelis opened her eyes, turned her head, fixed her gaze
into Elise's. "You're missing something?" she said, in her own
sharp voice.

"Yes!" said Elise.

"When was the last time you saw it?"

"I've never seen it."

"Something unseen. . . . " said Mrs. Lelis, with quietly ironic exaggaration, then, "This isn't a lost and found, you know." The nervous congregation took the laugh gratefully.

"You can help me, can't you?" said Elise, smiling now.

Mrs. Lelis glared, smiling tensely too. "Come see me," she said, "*after*." Elise nodded, accepting but not acquiescing. Dora felt relieved, for the moment.

Was Elise challenging the medium's realness? Or did she actually believe? It was hard to tell. She seemed quite at ease, sitting there watching the seance as though it were a show, smiling at the right places, looking serious when others did. Picking up where it left off after Elise's sudden demand, the service went back to its usual routine; someone's dead sweetheart showed up, and there was a long, emotional scene. Dora wanted to take her friend's hand again, but somehow couldn't find it in the right position to be taken.

When it was over, Elise walked on ahead up the aisle and greeted the Lelises, shaking their hands and saying what a lovely house, and what an interesting service. Then Mrs. Lelis lifted the curtain to the rear of the platform, inviting Elise to follow her behind it, which she did, leaving Dora all alone.

Dora sat, apprehensive, then bored, then increasingly amazed. Finally Elise came back out through the curtains. She looked happy, bright and untroubled.

"I'm sorry," she said. "I would've asked if you could come back too, but she just started talking so fast."

"'sall right."

They went upstairs and climbed into their galoshes.

"Well," said Elise, "at least I know where we have to go now."

"Where?"

"Germany. That's where he is."

"*He?*"

"Drosselmeyer."

They stepped out into the pretty white evening.

"It makes so much sense, I don't know why I didn't see it," said Elise excitedly. "The camera! It worked like a vacuum cleaner, he pointed it at me and it sucked the soul right out of me. That's what the Indians told her! They know! They never let people take their pictures, because they know there are people like Drosselmeyer and his rotten camera going around, stealing souls. *That's* what he did! That's why he ran away!

"After I got back from New Haven I tried to find him, I thought, that guy's got my last decent performance on that film he took. I wanted to get a print of it. But when I went to Astoria, they said he'd just left right after he'd made the test with me. Hopped on the boat to the old country, with me in a little can under his arm."

"That's not fair. That's your test as much as his. He should at least make you a copy."

"He should give me back what he took from me."

"So the spirits told you where to find him?"

"Not specifically. He probably went to Oofa. That's the big studio in Berlin."

Dora frowned.

"Isn't Berlin awful, though?" she said. "You have to have a wheelbarrow of money just to buy a loaf of bread."

"No, that was years ago. The inflation's over, it's more like it is here now. Only less gangsters around, because beer's still legal."

"Wonder how much it costs to get to Germany? Maybe I've got enough in the bank. . . . I wish I'd saved more."

Elise slipped her arm around her waist and kissed her.

"Maybe we could live with your Opa for a while," she said. "We could get jobs and save money until we had enough."

"Wouldn't you rather go back to New York? Try going back on stage?"

"No, it's no good. I can't work the way I am. Well, maybe I could. But I wouldn't want to be seen."

"Couldn't you just—"

"The thing is," said Elise, "it costs money to work in the

theater. You have to have nice hair and clothes, and you have to have money to live on, because they don't pay you much, unless you're a featured player. A lot of the girls had money of their own, or they had gentlemen friends."

"What did you do?" asked Dora with trepidation.

"I worked my head off, that's what I did. I'd do a walk-on in the first act at one theater, then I'd throw on my coat, run down the street to the next theater, get in costume for a bit as a maid, do my bit . . . good for my legs, all that running down Broadway . . . . But I got speaking parts when they finally heard my voice. Dora, wait till you see Broadway. You'll think you're in fairyland. The theaters are all dark wood and velvet, like jewel boxes. And the best ones are built so you can whisper and your voice will go all the way to the back of the balcony. And the people in the front rows sparkle with diamonds and sequins. And when you look at their faces, they move closer. They understand, they listen. That's never happened before to me. That's why I have to go to get my soul back, Dora. I want things to be the way they were. I have to be on that stage. It's the only place where I feel right."

Everything was closed—deadly New Year's Day was still in force—and the girls were dying for refreshment but didn't really want to go home yet. As they approached Uncle Ted's house, Dora thought they might stop in and beg a cup of tea, since his light was on. "Maybe he's not alone," said Elise.

"Of course he is," said Dora, "he doesn't have any friends."

Dora hadn't visited her Uncle Ted at home since Mutti stopped talking to him. The place where he was living now wasn't as nice as his old rooming house, but it was enormous. It took up the whole top floor of a house and had its own entrance up the back way. It had its own kitchen and bath, a parlor and two bedrooms, but Uncle Ted slept on a studio bed in the parlor. The other two rooms were for books.

"You'd think he'd get sick of them," said Elise.

"No, the books in the library are just the ones he works with. These are the ones he wants to live with."

Uncle Ted let them in. "Well, orphans of the storm," he said.

"Uncle Ted, can we have something hot to drink, please? We're half froze."

"Certainly. Something hot. . . . I've got some Postum."

"We'll make it, Mr. Krauss. Want some?"

They scrubbed out a kettle and some cups, and soon had the water simmering. "What are you girls doing out, anyway?" Uncle Ted asked.

"We went to church," said Elise.

"The Lelises," said Dora.

"That's not a church, it's a puppet show," said Uncle Ted. "Did they have the dancing tambourine?"

They drank the bitter Postum plain, as there wasn't any sugar and Uncle Ted's milk was old and unspeakable.

"So you're back from New York," Uncle Ted said to Elise.

"Just for a while. Till we can save enough money to go to Berlin."

"Really," said Uncle Ted, licking Postum from his moustache.

"I'll have to find out how much it costs. It probably wouldn't be much if we went in steerage."

"That sounds terrible. Why would you do that?"

"That's how you and Mutti came over, didn't you?" asked Dora.

"I don't think so," Uncle Ted said. "Your grandmother would never have taken us in steerage. She'd have been afraid of fleas."

"Anyway, I'm broke, so I'm going to need a job," said Elise. "Are they hiring at the library?"

"Very possibly."

"Maybe we could both work there," said Dora.

"You could," said Uncle Ted. "But the pay's peanuts."

"How about Losch's?" Elise asked.

"I quit," said Dora. "They're horrible."

"Just as well. I'd just get fat around all that ice cream."

"Oh, you don't want to EAT it after a while," said Dora. "It's terrible. Just cow fat and old frozen pistachios."

Uncle Ted tossed his empty Postum cup aside and crossed the room. "Berlin, huh," he said.

"We just really want to go there," said Dora, hoping that Elise wasn't going to say any more of that spooky Lelis stuff about souls.

"No reason why you shouldn't," said Uncle Ted. "What does your mother say?"

"We're not telling her," said Dora.

"How about your mother?" Uncle Ted asked Elise.

"She doesn't care. She's marrying my father."

"Huh," said Uncle Ted.

"You know," he said, "I have a friend in Berlin. I wonder, if you go there, if you could visit him. Very interesting fellow, well educated. Runs a book shop."

"Sounds just right for Dora," said Elise.

"Well, he is a widower, but he's a little old for you girls. Anyway, you wouldn't want to marry a German, would you?" he said, winking at Dora. "There's some books he's got I've been wanting to buy from him. Maybe you could bring them back for me."

"Love to," said Dora

"When were you girls thinking of going?"

"When we get the money together. Should take a while."

"I could give you money now. I mean, not now, not till Monday, when the bank's open. Then again I could write you a check."

"Oh my goodness," said Elise, "that's awfully nice of you, but we couldn't—"

"Sure you could."

"It would cost a lot," Dora said. "We'd have to get passports and things."

"Oh, I don't think it would be that expensive," said Uncle Ted. "American money goes a long way over there."

"Really," said Dora, thinking of the wheelbarrows full of Deutschmarks in a different way.

"I could write my friend and ask if he knows a place where you could stay in Berlin."

"That would be so nice, Uncle Ted!"

"All right, you plan your itinerary, and I'll write Mr. Süss."

"Oh, thank you! Thanks for the Postum, too."

"'s no trouble."

They hopped back into the snow, exhilarated.

"All right," said Elise, "now, to work."

They had to improve their German. Dora knew it backwards and forwards on paper, and both had learned to speak a little at home, but they had to have more than this if they were going to go to a strange city all by themselves. In the mornings and evenings they worked up in Dora's attic, bundled in comforters, but during the afternoons they'd make a little nest for themselves in a corner of Uncle Ted's office. Sometimes they tested their pronunciation and grammar out on him, if he wasn't too grumpy. Otherwise, they busied themselves with their researches. This was the second order of business.

"Is it in the camera, do you think?" Dora asked.

"That's what I wonder."

"Do you think it really was a camera?"

"That's what it looked like. It looked like this one," Elise said, pointing to one in a book.

"That's an old one."

"It's the silent type."

"He made a silent test? Without your voice? How stupid!"

"He didn't have the equipment. You have to have a whole studio setup, with the microphones and the camera in a special box so you won't hear the racket when it's running. It takes a lot of people to operate . . . but thank God he didn't do it that way! Even if he did get my soul, at least I've still got my voice!"

"What did he do with the film?"

"Probably kept it. If there *was* film."

"You think he had an empty camera?"

"Oh, I don't know, he could have had a voodoo doll in there. Dora, you're not just humoring me, are you? I know this all sounds demented."

"No. I don't know if I trust all that stuff Mrs. Lelis said. . . . but I know you, and something's not right with you, I can see it."

"I feel anemic."

"Your color isn't good. . . . Your hair's kind of flat."

"Don't you two sound cute," said Uncle Ted, "chattering over there like a couple of Krauts."

"But we are Krauts, Uncle Ted."

"You think so!" said Uncle Ted. "We'll see what the real ones say when they get a look at you."

*   *   *

What would happen to Turandot? Dora hated to leave her. But you can't just take a dog along when you go overseas. Even if you could smuggle her onto the boat, they'd probably find her when you passed through customs, and then she'd have to stay in quarantine, which took six months. Believing herself to be abandoned in dog prison, she might die of despair.

"She'd be all right at home, wouldn't she?" said Elise. "Your mother and grandfather wouldn't let her starve to death."

"They're awfully forgetful."

"Maybe we could bribe the customs people. Or maybe— wait a minute."

One of Elise's sewing fits came over her. This one was particularly inspired. She took Mutti's old sealskin coat and rigged it up with a sling pouch so Elise could carry Turandot in such a way that she appeared a bit stout and unfashionable, but not like a dog-smuggler necessarily.

"I think she really likes it," said Dora. "She's wagging her tail."

"No," said Elise sadly, "it's not going to work."

"Course it will!"

"No. It would work on stage. But not in life."

Dora realized she was right. Reluctantly, they lowered Turandot from her sling and stood watching as she investigated this strange, still animal she'd just been inside of.

"I'm sure they won't let her die," said Elise. "They kept you alive when you were little."

"I guess I'll have to trust them. But the minute we come back, we've got to get her."

"Of course we will."

"And I'm going to never never leave you again," Dora told Turandot, "I'm going to take you with me everywhere. *Everywhere.*"

"That's right," added Elise. "You're going to like being a New York dog. You'll go for walks in Central Park. And you'll have entree to all the best theaters. I'll see to that."

*　　*　　*

Uncle Ted showed them the letter he'd gotten back from his friend the Berlin bookseller—a quicker response than either he or the girls had been expecting. Mr. Süss thanked him for his generous proposition, and would be pleased to host the girls on their visit, for however long they wished. His sister, a doctor's widow, lived in a house in the Charlottenburg district where they'd be welcome to stay with her and Mr. Süss' stepson, who, like Elise, was just starting an illustrious career in the theater.

"Uh oh," said Elise. "Well, we can stick a chair under the doorknob at night."

The fact that Mr. Süss spoke fluent English (or at least wrote it) was a relief, as was the fact that he wasn't averse to associating with actors. "But then, that's Europe," said Dora. "They respect artists there."

"Don't pay as much, though," said Elise.

Uncle Ted took an early lunch hour, and helped them carry their bags to the train station, where he gave them a new Berlin Baedeker's he'd stolen for them from the backlog and an envelope full of money. "Now," he said, as the New York-bound train lowered its steps to the platform, "run for your lives, kids." And they did.

Chapter 7

As the train ran along the Hudson River, Dora fell in love with New York. Not the dreaded gray city that lurked like Charybdis waiting to suck them in at the end of the track, but the country on the riverside. With its red rocky cliffs and weeping trees, the crazy castle in the middle of the water, even Sing-Sing, the Hudson Valley countryside possessed a grave, stately beauty that the flat, deforested Midwestern landscape Dora had spent all her young life in hadn't prepared her for. No wonder the Dutchmen cheated the Indians out of this land with their beads, she thought; no wonder the rich still craved it.

"Look at the other side of the river," Elise told her. "That's where Helen Hayes and Charlie Chaplin live."

"Really!"

"That's where we'll live."

Dora's mouth opened in the biggest smile she'd had since she'd been a baby.

"We could live here?!" she exclaimed. "But wouldn't we have to live closer to Broadway?"

"We'd probably want to have a pied-a-terre in the city to stay in when I'm too tired to go home after a show. But we wouldn't want to live there *all* the time. I have a feeling you'll be happier in Nyack than Manhattan."

Much happier, thought Dora, as the dark city emerged at the end of the line. But the thought of living along the broad, silver river, frisking along the banks with Turandot and Charlie Chaplin, gentled her spirit so that her dread unexpectedly let go of her, and as the outskirts of New York City slowly piled up on either side of her she sat with equanimity, considering it all in perspective.

A soft flurry began so that by the time they were inside Manhattan it was frosted with snow like confectioner's sugar. A pretty golden light from the west made the concrete and brick glow cleanly, and Grand Central Station glittered like a palace as the good-naturedly disinterested conductors handed the girls down to the platform as though they were great ladies.

To spare themselves the horror of wrestling their baggage onto the subway they hired a taxi to the women's hotel where Elise herself had stayed her own very first night here. Poor Dora hadn't slept all night on the train, and was getting brown around the eyes and a little hysterical, so Elise installed her in their room for a nap while she went to buy their tickets for the boat.

Though the mattress was firm and the cotton sheets were crisp and thick and rough, the way she liked them, Dora was too overstimulated to lie down. She went to the window and looked out at the quiet street. It was Sunday afternoon, and most people were home fixing supper or reading the funny papers. The enormity of her surroundings made her smile, all the streets like these going on for miles instead of the ten blocks or so that constituted the tall part of her own city. She liked the height and heft of it, and the way the skyscrapers sheltered her from the stark winter sun. There was something agreeable about the closeness of this little room, with sounds coming from every side—an automobile on the street, a woman coughing behind the far wall, the sound of a tap running down the hall. She felt protected with all these signals of sentient beings nearby. She didn't feel like a stranger at all, why should she? New York was full of strangers, all in it together.

Elise came back and showed her the tickets. They were very handsome and substantial-looking, befitting the new German line that issued them. "Our ship's the Konstantin," said Elise. "The man said it's the most modern liner on the Atlantic. We'll be in Bremerhaven in a week."

"You're kidding! That's barely enough time to get seasick!"

They went down to a little diner around the corner from their hotel and had hamburgers and coffee. Then Dora felt sleepy, but Elise insisted on showing her around a little. "I want you to see my city, Dora. More than just the cement and train tracks. The part that's alive. You'll like it."

The lights were all on now, the neon tubing like will-o-the-wisps in the windows and over the doorways. "If we keep going this way, we'll be on Broadway," said Elise.

They got there as the evening's sleek clientele were milling along the streets and through the glass doors, picking up their tickets at the box offices. Enormous, ugly-elegant marquees shilled the attractions above the glossy rivers of silk hats and animal pelts. Now this was the New York that was most familiar from the comics and movies and magazines, and therefore the weirdest to see walking next to you. Dora was awestruck simply looking at the ladies' shoes.

Though most of what the marquees offered looked disappointingly stupid, they could make out the names Cornell and Lunt and Eugene O'Neill. "Let's see something!" said Elise.

"But I'm so tired, Elise. What if I fell asleep?"

"At least you'd have good dreams!"

They were about to go into the O'Neill show when Elise glanced up the street, cried out "JOUVET!" and ran, yanking Dora along after her. They wound up watching a Moliere play in the original French, which Elise had never studied and didn't understand twenty words of. Dora, who had seldom heard the language spoken herself and never in seventeenth century verse, nevertheless found herself able to follow the story, not so much by the words themselves but by the way the actors shaped and used them. The audience sat rapt as though listening to opera, with the great Louis Jouvet the star baritone. Tall, slender, vulpine, with eyes

like pale sapphires, he sang his lines rather than speaking them—
a peculiar technique he'd developed to mask his incurable stutter,
Elise whispered confidentially.

"I'm in love," murmured Dora, as the lights came up at intermission.

"You're supposed to be," replied Elise, her eyes wet and
bright, cheeks rose petal-red.

*   *   *

It's one thing to buy a ticket for a boat to Germany, but something
pretty different to actually stand on a concrete dock and look up
at this terrible hunk of steel, big as a bank building and looking
just about as able to stay afloat, and think, this thing is going to
go thousands of miles out into the sea, and I'm going to be in it.
If it had been only her, Dora would have turned and run right
back onto solid earth again. But she couldn't do that to Elise, so
she walked with her up the planks, knowing what the condemned
felt.

They didn't have steerage anymore, at least not on the
Konstantin. Instead, they had Tourist Cabin Third Class, which
was a little room with bunks on the wall and pipes on the ceiling,
snug enough for a fast crossing in February. It was below the
waterline, which Dora had read somewhere was the safest place
to be, and this made her feel a little better. With no portholes,
and a long climb up to the deck, at least she didn't have to be
reminded where she was. As for seasickness, they were well prepared. Dora had brought Dramamine and Coke syrup, and they
hadn't eaten breakfast that morning. When the final casting-off
signal bellowed, they positioned themselves on the floor of their
cabin with blankets and paper bags, and Dora started drilling
Elise on her German grammar. It actually kept them from getting
sick, up to a point.

"How the hell do they decide what sex things are?" Elise
snapped, in the middle of her declensions.

"I don't see any system to it," said Dora. "In French it's easier to guess, but then you've got a fifty-fifty chance of being right even if you aren't sure. Throwing the neuters in is what really trips you up."

"The minute I start trying to talk to them they're going to laugh me out of the country."

"No they won't. They're just going to correct you. You know how Germans are."

Sure enough, the minute they were well enough to leave their cabin, people started correcting them.

Chapter 8

They arrived at Bremerhaven safe and on schedule, and got right on the train to Berlin. All Dora could think about was getting somewhere where she could feel the earth again, steady and unmoving under her feet.

So this was the Old Country. It looked very much like where they'd come from, only with many more trees, and many more little cottages and farms and villages packed into the rolling, frozen landscape, where picturesque patches of snow decorated the brown meadow-bottoms and hilltops. It was strange to see so much wooded land with so few tree stumps. But of course, Dora realized, they didn't have to cut down so many trees here; they'd already built all their houses and barns and churches centuries ago, while all the people back home were really just getting started, hewing their woods into cities and towns.

Presently, the outer suburbs of the city started to cluster around them, and as Berlin itself hove into view, Dora felt herself chuckling in delight. What a dear little city! Like a toy New York!

She felt Elise nudge her. "Dora," she murmured to her in English, "I can tell what these people are saying."

"Told you so!" Dora whispered.

It was a pleasure to hear, the rich, gruff, rolling cadences, like Opa's, all around them. This wasn't at all what she'd felt a foreign country would be like. She'd expected to feel, well, *for-*

eign. But everyone looked like her, everyone was dressed like her, albeit a little duller perhaps, more staid and elegant.

Mr. Süss had told them which trolley to catch, which stop to look for, how far to go once they got off, and where to turn. They were such precise directions that they found the house without any trouble at all. It was a handsome old row house, not rich, but comfortable. There was a maid, too. Dr. Kleinzach must have done very well to leave his wife in such circumstances, considering it wasn't long ago people here had to go around with wheelbarrows full of money just to buy a sack of potatoes. And Mrs. Kleinzach looked healthy and happy, and not in the least deprived.

"I hope you'll pardon me for speaking German," said Mrs. Kleinzach. "I'm sorry I don't know any English!"

"I just hope you'll excuse my terrible German," said Dora.

"You're doing very well! How about your friend, does she know much German?"

"She's learning. Do you understand what we're saying, Elise?"

"A little," said Elise.

"Well," said Mrs. Kleinzach, "let me know if I'm talking too fast. And I'll let you know if you make any mistakes!"

The hired girl brought tea and cookies. They were really getting very chummy.

"My uncle told us that your nephew is an actor," said Elise.

"Don't worry about Felix," replied Mrs. Kleinzach. "I made him find somewhere else to stay."

"I'm sorry. We didn't intend to put him out of his room! "

"Oh, not at all! There's plenty of room, but it wouldn't be proper for him to be living here with two young girls in the house. It's better this way. With the crazy hours he keeps, I had to tiptoe around all day so I wouldn't wake him, and then in the middle of the night he'd be dragging in his half-starved friends for a meal. Though I didn't mind, really. I love the theater, I think he's very brave to be in it, it's a terrible life. Like being a lion tamer or something. Is it like that in America, Elise? Do you understand what I'm saying?"

"A little," said Elise.

"Oh!" laughed Mrs. Kleinzach. "You'll learn, you'll learn!"

*   *   *

The question of how a young lady goes about reclaiming her soul had been the subject of much discussion between the girls. The most obvious and civilized thing would be to send Drosselmeyer a politely worded request, and wait for a response. Back home Elise had in fact written to him in care of the studio where the trade papers had announced he was making his film, but had gotten no response. She posted another letter the day they'd arrived in Berlin, letting him know she was in town and where she'd be staying. Maybe he'd be kind enough to send a delivery boy to Mrs. Kleinzach's to return the film with Elise's soul in it, in which case the rest would be very easy. They could collect Uncle Ted's books from Mr. Süss's shop, go on to Vienna, which Dora was dying to visit, perhaps take a side trip to Paris if the money went that far, and then hop on a French steamer and tourist third class it back to New York and a glorious future on the Hudson. But neither girl expected Drosselmeyer to be this reasonable. They would probably have to track him down in his lair, rob and perhaps even murder him. But whatever was necessary must be done, as Elise's life couldn't progress without its motive force, and Dora had no illusions of there being any future for herself apart from what Elise might lead her into. While they pondered their dark alternatives, munching schnecken in Mrs. Kleinzach's parlor, the first truly great man of the theater that either had met came into their lives.

In essence Felix had all the features of a simply handsome young man. But as though through some trick of optical distortion he was all disproportionate, chubby and stunted, no taller than little Elise herself, and his huge brown eyes bulged dangerously. He had a sweet little cleft in his chin and a dimple in his cheek when he laughed.

"He's a full-blooded Jew, just like Jesus," Mrs. Kleinzach said proudly.

And he wasn't shy at all. "Mama, what pretty American girls!" he said. "Can they understand what we say?"

"The dark one doesn't much. But little Dora speaks German better than you do."

"Do you!" exclaimed Felix, smiling and moving nearer.

"Are you the actress?" he asked Dora.

"No, *she* is."

"Oh, you poor little thing."

He took Elise's hand and gazed at her.

"You have beautiful eyes," he said.

"So have you," said Elise.

"Thank you. So you've just arrived in Berlin? Have you been to the theater here yet?"

"No."

"Well, you'll go tonight. There's a new production that's just opened at the Schauspielhaus, I'm told I'm very good in it. You'll be my guest, and we can have supper afterwards. And Mama Kleinzach will come as your chaperone, won't you, Mama?"

"Ohhh, no," said Mrs. Kleinzach, "that one, I couldn't bear to see again! Why don't you take the girls with you to the theater and show them around backstage?"

"That's a good idea. That way Elise can see how we do things here. Is it true that you've played on Broadway, Elise?"

"Yes."

"Enviable creature! Well, tonight I'm going to take you to my Broadway. The Kurfürstendamm, it's called."

"I know," said Elise.

"You clever girl. How much *do* you know about this place you've come so far to see? We'll just have to find out, won't we?"

*   *   *

The more adventurous sort of modern theater hadn't come as far west as where Dora had done most of her theatergoing, and so what went on in the Schauspielhaus came as a shock to her. Elise herself hadn't ever seen anything so artistic. The play itself, which had to do with the surging erotic desires of youth, left them both bugeyed. You could get away with an awful lot here without the police coming to raid you. Mind you, it was done with impressive style.

At first they wondered whether they were in the wrong theater because they couldn't find Felix's name anywhere in the program. "Maybe he's a walk-on," said Elise.

But he had told them he would be playing the second male lead. It was confusing, as the actor credited with the role in the program was Kurt Ross. Maybe Felix was the understudy, and had to go on tonight?

"No," said Elise, "that's his part all right. He must be Kurt Ross."

By whatever name, Felix or Kurt Ross, it was an extraordinary creature who appeared on the raked stage before them. Nothing the least actorly about him, certainly more natural-seeming than the striving, posing youngsters around him. Yet every gesture was wrought with keen concentration, as though he were a master puppeteer, manipulating with dexterous care the funnily articulated members of his own little form in the most cunning, unexpectedly nonchalant manner imaginable. You watched him breathless, marveling at his ingenuity. It was riveting to witness. So real!

After the curtain calls they trotted right backstage—Elise seemed to know the way—and found Felix, damp, full of filthy-looking makeup and very merry, surrounded by excited young women, some of them very pretty. And yes, they were calling him Kurti.

"My little Americans!" he cried when he saw them. Wriggling free of his admirers, he scooped Elise and Dora into his arms. "Did you understand the show?"

"No," said Elise. "You were wonderful."

He kissed her and hugged her.

"It's a very dirty show, isn't it?" he asked Dora.

"I liked it," said Dora. "It's truthful."

"Yes, God knows."

He excused himself and went into his dressing room. The other females glared at Dora and Elise and sussurated among themselves. Elise gave Dora a cigarette and they shared a match. They felt very, very grown up.

Felix emerged quickly wearing a clean elegant suit, his fresh, chubby face shiny from its rubdown of cold cream. "Mama Kleinzach said to bring you girls straight home," he said. "Would you like to go straight home or would you like to go to Mutzbauer's for some nice dumplings?"

They went to Mutzbauer's and ate an enormous meal— though, to Felix's chagrin, Dora refused to drink anything but lemonade—and then Felix suggested they go dancing, but they were too sleepy. So he took them home in a taxi.

"I'm disappointed," he told them. "I thought you might be homesick and want to hear a little jazz."

"We don't really like jazz," said Elise.

"*You don't like jazz?*"

"It's sort of nasty," said Dora.

"What sort of music do you like?"

"Good music," said Dora. "I don't like the new stuff much, I'm old-fashioned. I'd rather listen to Strauss than Stravinsky."

"Oh, my God," said Felix. "Trapped in the back of a taxi with two National Socialists!"

"I'm starting to get the hang of this language," Elise told Dora later, in bed. "I can even understand Felix now. I don't know why he talks like that, have you noticed? Kind of funny and blurry."

"That's a Viennese type accent he's got. He must've come

from somewhere east of Germany, they all talk like that. They sound to regular Germans like Southerners sound to us."

"Ugh! Well, his diction is much better when he's on stage. I'm glad we got to see him. I bet he'll be famous someday. What a little firecracker!"

"It must make you sad. To see him up there where you want to be."

"Sort of. But that's the way the show world works. Some nights you're on, some nights you're off. That's why they call it 'Variety,' not "The Same Old Damn Thing.'"

"Hope we can get to Drosselmeyer soon."

"I think we will."

"I was thinking maybe Felix could help."

"I can't imagine why else he's here."

"You're right!"

"Yes! That's what Mrs. Lelis told me. She said, when your cart comes to the mountain, the path will appear."

"Mmm . . ."

"Yes. He may be our path, God help us."

Chapter 9

It was very late when they got in, and Elise slept in much later than she'd intended to. When she got up, she found Mrs. Kleinzach eating her breakfast while Dora sat bolt upright in front of her untouched coffee with eyes wide as her saucer. "Too bad that naughty Felix kept you up so late!" said Mrs. Kleinzach. "The most beautiful man called for you just half an hour ago."

"It was Drosselmeyer," Dora said dazedly.

"It certainly was," smiled Mrs. Kleinzach, and showed her the card he left. It was pale greenish grey engraved with a very modern typeface. On the back he'd written *Come at midnight*. "He's a VERY busy man," said Mrs. Kleinzach.

"Mrs. Kleinzach looked up the address," said Dora. "We could walk there from here."

"Did he tell you to come?"

"He sort of looked at me."

It was only nine-thirty; they had nearly fifteen hours to wait. What hideous torture! But to have it all over so easily was nothing to sneeze at. Besides, it gave them the day free to explore the city, and to pick up Uncle Ted's books.

Mr. Süss's antiquarian bookshop was in downtown Berlin, on one of the side streets off Unter den Linden. Elise avoided used book shops herself, as she hated the smell. But Dora glowed at first sight of the little shop. Peeking in the window, she went "Ooh!" and "ooh!" and "oooh!"

"Don't spend all your Uncle Ted's money!" said Elise.

"Oh, I don't think I could afford these—that's a first edition of Grimm! I can't believe he put it in the window, it'll get all faded. I'll have to tell him."

A small, balding, hideous little man with the most enchanting smile Elise had ever seen came to the door. "And this is your friend, Miss Dora?" he asked.

"Mr. Süss!" cried Dora. "What a beautiful store!"

They made their introductions, and followed Mr. Süss to his little kitchen over the shop, where he put on the coffee pot.

"Do you speak German?" he asked Elise.

"I'm learning," said Elise.

"Very good! I hear you went to see Felix last night."

"Yes, he's wonderful."

Mr. Süss winced with pride, made a funny, twirly gesture.

"Why does he call himself Kurt Ross?" asked Dora. "I don't think he needs a stage name. Felix Süss is a beautiful name."

"Well, it's not Felix Süss, actually, it's Felix Zuzloff," said Mr. Süss, making a sour mouth. "When I married his mother, he insisted on keeping his father's name. Well, that's as it should be. And taking my name wouldn't do him much good . . . Some producer gave him the name Ross. It's not bad."

"Sounds American," said Dora.

"He loves America. All the time he was growing up, all he was interested in was Hollywood movies and cowboy stories."

"What does his mother think of him changing his name?"

"We lost her when Felix was still just a little fellow . . . ah, well," said Süss, pushing the subject away with a shrug. "What's in a name, eh? Felix is happy in what he's doing, that's what would matter to her."

Surprisingly, Mr. Süss made better coffee than his sister did, mellow and compelling. Their heads buzzed a little as he showed them more of the treasures that had so tantalized Dora.

"Mr. Süss," Dora said at last, "before I forget, we might as well get those books while we're here."

"Oh, no, Miss Dora, that's not necessary. I'll bring them to you when you're ready."

"Well, we might be leaving soon."

"How soon? I thought you'd be staying at least a month."

"Oh, not that long!"

"You'd come all this way just to stay for a day or two? Oh, no," said Mr. Süss, "there's more to Berlin than that! Besides, your uncle's been very generous with Mrs. Kleinzach about your room and board."

"It's so nice of her to have us."

"Mrs. Kleinzach loves visitors. And so do I. Anyway, your uncle's ordered a lot of books, they're too heavy for you to carry through the streets. You don't want to be lumbered with a lot of old boxes. I could bring them myself to the ship when you go. It's no trouble at all, believe me! Your uncle is one of my favorite customers."

"Uncle Ted would scream if he saw what he was doing to those books," said Dora, as they rounded the corner onto Unter den Linden. "Half of them ought to be in quarantine. They're full of mold and bugs . . . it's going to spread to all the other books. And it's FILTHY in there, did you notice, the dust? That's really bad for books! It can rub the bindings right off."

"You ought to be a librarian, Dora."

"You have to go to college for that."

"No!"

"Sure you do, Uncle Ted did."

"Maybe you should go to college. You might like it."

"I probably would, but you have to finish high school first."

"I don't know why you didn't. You didn't have much to go."

"I just couldn't. I couldn't stand having to sit there with the teacher talking at me. I felt like I was smothering, I wanted to scream. All I could think of was getting out."

"It was pretty boring at that."

"My grades were all horrible anyway. I just couldn't seem to get anything through my head. It was like I stopped being able to learn. But what's strange is, when we were reading that German grammar on the boat, I felt fine. It was no trouble at all. I remembered things I hadn't even realized I'd learned before."

"I guess that's the way I am. In school everything was so hard. But now I'm out I can read Shakespeare, I can even read that German stuff, and it's not any harder than reading a magazine. I understand things right away. Maybe we're smarter now?"

"Maybe that's what they really mean by 'growing up,'" replied Dora. "Your brains finally get big enough."

*   *   *

It actually was rather a long walk from their side of town to Drosselmeyer's, and it wasn't an easy route to follow in the dark, not to mention someone having made off with a crucial street sign. But they didn't make any mistakes in following Mrs. Kleinzach's directions, and even got there a little early. It was a very pretty modern villa, geometric and functional as was the style here, but the red brick and evergreen shrubbery indicated a certain affable traditionalism. Dora sensed right away that Mr. Drosselmeyer had probably been lent this residence by a friend.

A sleepy old woman let them in and led them to a drawing room where Drosselmeyer, on seeing them, rose from his armchair and gave that little funny jump that aristocratic German males made in the movies. Dora was startled at the height of him. She was frankly expecting a stout little fellow with a shaved head like Erich von Stroheim, but here was a man more on the order of Jouvet, six feet and more, with blue eyes and wavy ash-blond hair. The effect of him expanding to full length as they approached him was a little frightening, like a big horse rearing up at them.

"Good evening, Miss Elise, Miss Dora," he said, in his deep, flat voice. Dora, startled he remembered her name, put out her hand to shake his; he actually bowed over it, and did his little bounce again.

My goodness, he doesn't look Jewish, was Dora's thought. Could Elise have been wrong? But then there were Jews with blue eyes. What did they call them, Sephardic? Anasazi? Ashanti? He held out his hand, his fingers tilted graciously in the direction of the couch where they should sit. Elise ogled his smoking jacket, an ugly-lovely abstract pattern in maroon, gray and gold satin, the sort of garment she herself might have run up for a fellow actor in one of her plays back home.

"Miss Elise, I read your letter but wasn't quite sure how to respond," Drosselmeyer began. "What is it you want from me exactly?"

"I tried to make it clear to you," said Elise, "I'm sorry if I didn't. Should I explain again?"

"Please."

"I want to know, what did you do with my film?"

"You mean my film, the one I wanted to use you for. That's been shelved. I've got to finish with the one I'm doing out here for Oofa first."

"I mean, my film."

"Oh, you mean *film*!"

He got up, excused himself, and left the room. Dora was dying to look around the room, but Elise kept to the edge of her cushion, legs and arms braced as if ready to jump to her feet but for the moment unmoving, except for a little tremor of muscle. So Dora kept put too.

Before too much longer Drosselmeyer trotted back with a small film can in his long, slender hand. He brought it to Elise, set it in her lap, drew off the cover and picked the reel out of its tin dish. He pulled the long black leader aside and held up the attached strip of frames to the light so that they could see the little sooty negative Elises printed there in black and gray.

"You're giving this to me?" asked Elise.

"For four thousand marks it's yours."

AR

"That's ridiculous," said Elise.

"It's a fair price," said Drosselmeyer. "And it's marks, not dollars."

"How do I know it's the real negative?"

"You could show it to anyone who knows about such things and they'd tell you it's the original," said Drosselmeyer, reclining back in his chair. "But why should it matter?"

"You know."

Drosselmeyer noddded. His right hand fussed with something on the other side of the chair's arm, making a soft crackle.

"So when you said that felt your soul was on the negative," said Drosselmeyer, "you weren't being poetic, you really meant. . . . "

The crackle came from some cellophane he had in his hand, tearing strips of it from something below their line of vision, balling it up as he went.

"Dear God," he said, "I'm in a Hermann Prinz film. Miss Elise, I assure you that if I did steal your soul, it was by accident. I didn't know such a thing was possible. But if it's true, I apologize."

"Then you'll give it back?"

"Yes, for four thousand marks, just as I told you."

During Drosselmeyer's struggle with the cellophane, it became apparent that he was unwrapping what looked like a very nice one-pound box of chocolates. Dora's mouth watered. She hadn't had a chocolate since she'd quit Losch's.

"I can't give you four thousand marks," said Elise.

"Of course you can."

"It's too much."

Drosselmeyer slipped a rich brown oblong between his full lips, and chewed ruminatively.

"Too much for your soul, dear girl?" he said moistly. "I couldn't possibly ask for less. I'd be insulting you."

Elise stood up. Dora thought she saw the cloth on her back twitch, like Turandot's fur when she saw a cat.

"And since it's the original negative, and I don't have any

prints," Drosselmeyer said, rising too, "you'd better take care of it, and for God's sake don't smoke while you're handling it; I saw a man blow his face off that way."

Drosselmeyer saw them out, as the old woman had gone to bed. He insisted on giving them the rest of the chocolates to take home. "Please give my respects to Mrs. Kleinzach," he said, "a very nice lady."

"I don't suppose you can give me a job," said Elise.

"I'm sorry, there's nothing available on the picture I'm doing now. But come to Babelsburg tomorrow morning. There's usually a call for extras."

"Extra work," muttered Elise.

"Miss Elise, you know there are no small parts, just small actors. Like yourself." He patted her cheek.

They tottered towards home, feeling dizzy and sleepy and humiliated. Dora peeked in the chocolate box. "Don't eat those," said Elise. "They're probably poison."

"He ate one."

"Well, it wouldn't hurt HIM. Rappacini's Son."

Dora sniggered.

"I bet they're liqueur chocolates. He probably keeps them around to get girls drunk."

"I hope not! I kind of wanted one."

"Go ahead, I was just kidding."

They were fondant-based, and heavenly.

"Maybe Uncle Ted could lend us the money," Dora said.

"No, I couldn't ask him for more money, he'd get the wrong idea about us. I'll just have to go to work and earn it, that's all. Lucky you don't need a soul to do film work."

Chapter 10

Dora was beginning to think Berlin was the sweetest little city imaginable. It was just as modern as New York, though of course much older in some places, and the buildings were small enough so the sun could still come through to the pavement, and the air was much fresher than it was at home. There were less factories and soot, so the bricks were cleaner and the ladies could wear winter white. "I think I like this better than New York," said Dora.

"It's not bad!" said Elise.

So without complaint they settled in at Mrs. Kleinzach's and, taking Drosselmeyer's advice, went to try out for work as extra girls at Ufa. Thanks to beginner's luck and the two exquisite party frocks Elise had chosen from her costume trunk for them to wear to the studio, both girls were picked as set decorations for a scene involving a dapper actor with a receding hairline whom neither girl had ever heard of, and thus were relieved of the strain of being impressed by his presence among them. The actor took a special liking to Dora with her cute American accent, and gave her one of his monogrammed cigarettes to smoke. Other than that, it was an excruciatingly boring day's work. "All you do is sit around while they play with the lights!" said Dora.

"The theater's like that, too," said Elise. "Especially in rehearsal, there's big long stretches where nothing's happening, or you don't know what's going on and you could just die from nothing to do. But you've got to be ready when they need you."

"It's probably a lot different when you're a star."

"Not really. Only you get scared or annoyed on top of being bored. You just learn to use the time to prepare for when you're on, because that's the only thing that matters."

"I guess it doesn't matter to me."

"No, acting's a special sort of sickness, it's lucky only one of us has it. But I don't know if I could do this alone. I can understand what they're saying pretty well about half the time, and watching you and the other girls and doing what you're doing sort of fills in the rest, but I don't think I know enough German to really take direction."

"Why should you have to know the language to be in a silent picture?"

"I suppose I could fake my way around doing extra work. But I'm not going to make four thousand marks this way."

"No, but they might like your faking enough to make you a movie star."

"With this face?"

"Drosselmeyer likes it."

"Drosselmeyer is crazy. I don't know why he asked for that money. You saw that house, he doesn't need money!"

"You don't know, he could be really broke. Maybe that negative's the only thing he has, and he told you four thousand marks because he thought you'd get discouraged and go away."

"But he must be making money on this new picture he's doing."

"Maybe it's not enough. Maybe he's some sort of adventurer like Cagliostro who goes around tricking people, pretending he's rich and powerful when he's really just living by the seat of his pants."

The new camera set-up was ready, and they were called on to be intermittently amused and enchanted by their leading man for another twenty minutes. But there were technical problems, and since it was already five-thirty they sent them home, under orders to return in thirteen hours with the same costumes, which at present were disgusting as a result of having spent the day clinging to a pair of perspiring young bodies in constant proximity to searing lights and cigar fumes. Elise borrowed some things from Mrs. Kleinzach and showed Dora how to sponge down and rehabilitate a costume, to make it bearable for the wearer for another day.

"If you wonder why actresses wear so much eau de cologne, this is why," said Elise.

Fortunately for the girls and the dresses, their work at Ufa was done by mid-morning the next day. Though it hardly paid anything, it did make sense for an actress to act if there was work to be had, and so Dora obligingly went with Elise on her next call to Babelsburg. This time however the casting director was unimpressed by Dora's delicate features, but intrigued by Elise's bold ones. What could they do? Elise wasn't in a position to ask that Dora be let onto the set as her interpreter, so she hoped for the best and waved her goodbye, having ascertained she had enough fare for the trip home.

Dora waited nervously all day for Elise's return, feeling better as each hour passed. "God, please, please, let her work," she thought. "Even if it's only silly pantomime, it keeps her mind off her soul, and that's what matters. Please don't let her jump in front of a train!"

A merry Elise danced into the house just in time for supper that evening. "What a farce!" she said. "I got on the set, the assistant started talking to us, and in two seconds I was lost, totally disoriented, scared to death. They were looking at me like I was crazy, because everything I tried to do was wrong, so I had to confess—but I couldn't remember the words, they didn't know what I was saying! Finally the director came by and started asking me questions in AMERICAN. Thank Christ! He was wonderful, he got me all calmed down and had them give me a cup of tea, and then he asked me to give him a call when I knew the language a little better. He gave me his card." She gave it to Dora. "Do you know who this is?"

"Oh, my God," said Dora.

"Oh, yes," said Elise. "And he was nice to me."

They went and told Mrs. Kleinzach. "God in Heaven!" she exclaimed. "Maybe we'll have a big star in this house after all!"

* * *

So Dora resumed her intensive tutoring of Elise, with help from books Mr. Süss found for them. Felix offered to help her with pronunciation, but Mrs. Kleinzach said "No, then she'll pick up that terrible accent of yours and get all mixed up. Anyway, Dora has a better vocabulary." She took on the task of coaching both girls, with the result that they developed not only authentic Berlin accents, but genuine Berlin attitudes of speech that made it much easier to get on with the natives than had the literary German of the textbooks.

Mrs. Kleinzach admired the workmanship of Elise's handmade garments, especially those dresses they'd worn on their first film job. Knowing that the girl needed something to occupy herself besides the awesome task of doing justice to the great German language, she commissioned her to make a new dressing gown for her, and was so impressed by what Elise created for her that she asked if she could make something nice that she could wear to the theater when Felix's new play opened. "Maybe even along the line of *those* dresses," she said, meaning the ones Elise and Dora had worn in that scene in the film *Der Lustknabe*, "but of course more suitable for a woman my age," she said. Elise asked her to take her on the rounds of the better fabric stores, and boldly selected for her a queenly purplish velveteen that made her cheeks and eyes glow like a girl of thirty's. The drapery was essentially the same as that of the gown Elise had worn, which was fitting as both she and Mrs. Kleinzach were full-bosomed and generously hipped, only the long hem was lapped in such a way as to reveal glimpses of the older woman's still-exquisite calves. "Mama Kleinzach, are you looking for a new husband?" asked Felix, when they went backstage to kiss him after his first night (another triumph as another anguished young man, a funny one this time.)

Dora and Elise gave him a gift, a fancy muffler made with a remnant of Mrs. Kleinzach's gown. Elise had also sent backstage a card with a note that quoted, in English, Dorothy Parker's notorious salute to an actress friend: "A hand on your opening and may your parts grow bigger."

"I don't understand this," said Felix.

"It's an American good luck saying," said Elise. "Like having someone spit on your back."

"Well, thank you, I think it worked!"

In fact, Felix kept careful track of that note, and made sure it was on his dressing room table on every opening night and every first day of shooting he was engaged in thereafter. When he died it was found in a special silver case among the contents of his pockets that he'd set out the night before. The velvet scarf later turned up among the effects of his first wife's estate.

*   *   *

In the world of artists, things happen that only happen to ordinary people in dreams. One morning Elise was buying some cigarettes when she noticed Hermann Prinz step in line behind her. She was dazed with excitement, but out of instinctive politeness tried to be nonchalant and pretend she didn't notice who he was. Still, she felt as though he was looking at her. She caught his eye; he smiled, and she smiled.

"You're the little girl Drosselmeyer filmed in New York, aren't you?" he said.

Have you seen the test? she asked, and he said, I thought half of Berlin had seen it, it's the best thing Drosselmeyer's ever done, better than what he's doing now from what I've heard. What brings you here, and could you meet me for tea this Thursday? he asked.

Elise rode home from Babelsburg, half-dreaming and aching with pleasure. She ran home from the trolley stop, eager to find Dora and celebrate with her. But Dora wasn't home yet from the bookstore, where she'd been helping Mr. Süss set things to rights lately. So Elise went downtown to meet her, but she wasn't there, either.

"Felix came by an hour ago," said Mr. Süss. "He had a car he wanted to show off. I thought he'd driven her home in it."

But when Elise got back to Mrs. Kleinzach, there was no sign of Dora, even though it was nearly time for dinner. They waited for her until they grew so hungry they went ahead and ate without her. Feeling cross and out of sorts, Elise went up to her room afterwards to lie down and wait for Dora to come home.

She woke up hours later, still in her clothes. She heard sniggering and scuffling outside her open window. Down below she could see the tops of two heads, Dora's and Felix's. He was chasing her around the garden; she eluded him easily, but then he looked rather drunk.

Elise went straight down to the garden. Looking at them face to face, she saw to her relief that while Felix was definitely tipsy Dora was merely delirious with mischief.

"Where have you been all night?" Elise demanded.

"We've been in town," said Felix, softly and hoarsely, because he was so out of breath.

"What were you doing with her?"

"What? We were just . . . dancing. You know. At places where people do such things. I was teaching her how to dance like an American."

"He taught me to black bottom," said Dora.

"Let's show her," said Felix.

Felix counted out the beats, then started taking her through the steps, deliberately. He did it very well, with feeling; Dora just scrambled around a little and giggled.

"Felix, I hope to God Mrs. Kleinzach doesn't find out about

this," said Elise. "If she finds out you brought her home this late she'll be beside herself."

"I'm sorry," said Felix.

"You should be," said Elise, sniffing Dora suspiciously.

"'Don't worry, I didn't get her drunk," Felix said. "Your friend doesn't like French champagne, you know that? She says she likes ice cream sodas better. Let me come in for a minute, Elise."

"It's too late, Felix. Go home."

"Hey, this used to be my house!"

Elise shut the door in his shocked face, locked and bolted the door. Dora obediently followed her upstairs, and under her friend's watchful eye quietly got into her nightie, washed up and got into bed. Elise lay down next to her.

A few minutes later, Elise got up again and looked out the window, which overlooked the garden. Felix was still there. Elise couldn't resist shouting a stage whisper down to him: *"Hey!"*

Felix looked up, all sad Jewish eyes and Viennese wistfulness.

"Call me but love and I'll be new baptized!" hissed Elise, then slammed down the window sash. When she peeked out again a couple of minutes later he was gone.

Chapter 11

Having Dora in the book shop definitely drew in the customers. Better yet, because of her precocious knowledge of world history and culture, not to mention High German, she was able to make intelligent recommendations, which were invariably purchased. Best of all, with a female in residence, there was no more sweeping or coffee-making to be done, and dust was becoming a thing of the past. Already Mr. Süss' washerwoman had remarked on how many fewer handkerchiefs he used now.

"Here," he said one night, after the money in the till was counted and secured. He gave Dora a little bundle of bills. "Your sales commission, plus a small retainer," he said.

"Mr. Süss, it's not necessary. . . . "

"No, I've already written to your uncle and told him there's no need to send any money from now on. You've more than earned your keep, and it's only right that I pay you for the work you've done here."

"But it's no trouble. I like working here."

"When you like your work you do it well. And this is the work for you, my girl. Who ever saw a kid your age who cared so much about old books?"

"Well, I care if they're *good* books!"

"Mrs. Kleinzach was right," Mr. Süss said, as they strolled up the street, squinting against the warm amber of the setting sun. "The first day you and your friend came here, she said to me, 'Those girls are going to be good as gold to us, you'll see!'

And it's true. I've never seen that house so cheerful, even her cooking's improved—please, don't tell her I said that!

"Oh, look what those idiots did," he muttered. And he stopped and spat in his hand, and rubbed at the stone front of a beautiful little house where someone had chalked the crooked cross and the words, "Jew, why are you living here?"

"You have mixed neighborhoods, I think that's nice," said Dora, tactfully. "Back home people pretty much keep to themselves."

*   *   *

Tea with Hermann Prinz was bliss. Elise never forgot the things he told her that first afternoon together; years afterwards, she'd pass them on to younger actors, nearly word for word as he'd said them:

"Never refuse an autograph, even if you're tired and your hand aches. If they smile at you, smile too, but don't look them in the eye. Though if they stare at you and it makes you nervous, try staring back till they look away. It works with people just as well as animals!

"If you don't want to be bothered what you should do is carry a little dog about with you. People are afraid of dogs, especially those little ones with the pushed-in faces!

"A woman doesn't have to be beautiful at your age. The important thing is to keep yourself up so that you look well at fifty. Then everyone will say: What a great beauty she must have been!

"Don't bother with a press agent. Never trust a business manager. What you need is a talented lawyer, a competent tax accountant, a secretary who's literate and doesn't drink, and reliable household staff who won't steal from you. Before you sign anything, read it over, and if you don't understand it, ask somebody who does and who doesn't have any reason to lie to you about it. If it has anything to do with money, you must take care of it yourself, even if you have to spend two hours every night going over stacks of papers. It may be boring but I can't impress on you enough how necessary it is for you to know for yourself how much is coming in and where it is going to. Never let anyone else sign your checks or fiddle with your bank accounts or investments. Even the best people can't resist if you put temptation like that in their hands. And I'm sorry to say, the people who hover about actors are not the best people.

"If anyone asks you for anything, anything, tell them, I'll see. Just that: I'll see. Then, don't give it to them if you can help it!

"Don't drink anything stronger than wine, and never more than two glasses a day. Alcohol makes you older faster than anything else. It ruins your skin, your digestion, your concentration. Worst of all, it weakens your bladder, and that's disaster if you're working in the theater!

"Don't let them take pictures of you naked.

"Always be polite to journalists, and be extra nice to photographers. I needn't tell you why!"

It was also from Hermann that she first learned Felix's secret.

"That wonderful boy," said Hermann, "it's sad, for all his genius, to lose his soul like that."

Sensitive as he was, he saw right away the look on Elise's face, and changed the subject.

But it wasn't long after that that Elise realized she'd misunderstood Hermann's remark. More and more, she heard people saying "Poor Felix." Knowing that she lived with Felix's aunt, one bold little starlet asked if Felix had tried taking a cure. Then, Elise finally thought she understood, but she needed confirmation. The next time she saw Hermann she said to him in a quiet moment, "You know, I have to tell you, for a long time I didn't know about Felix."

"I didn't either," said Hermann eagerly, "until—" And then he told her, down to every last morsel, the gossip he'd heard about Felix's morphine addiction. The official story was that an irresponsible doctor had gotten him started on it while he was recovering from an appendectomy. Others said it was a dissolute girlfriend who'd introduced him to the habit. Interestingly, it was said that there wasn't a single needle mark to be found on him, anywhere that anyone had seen, on the beach, at the shvitz baths, backstage in dressing rooms, even in bed. But there was more than one theory, Hermann said, that would explain this.

It was dizzying, to think of anyone of her acquaintance being an actual dope fiend, least of all this bright-eyed, merry little dumpling—she was glad that Mrs. Kleinzach had turned him out of the house before they'd moved in, especially because of Dora. And then she was sad and ashamed, because in his condition there was probably no better place for him to stay than with his adoring step-aunt. How was poor Felix now? Where was he staying, and what other disgusting things might be happening to him?

Chapter 12

"I wonder how that boyfriend of yours in Transylvania is doing?" Elise asked Dora as they were washing their faces one morning.

"You know, I've no idea. I haven't written to him in ages."

"We should drop in on him sometime. It's not too terribly far from here. Supposed to be beautiful country."

"Stokes says they're all afraid of Dracula," said Dora.

"I wouldn't be, if he looked like Bela Lugosi!" said Elise.

"It's true though! It's very backward country, up in those mountains. Anyway, I don't think I could stand going up there. Heights make my stomach feel queer."

"It would be nice if you wrote to him anyway. He doesn't even know we're here, does he?"

"You're right!" said Dora. Later that morning, she found a nice picture postcard of the Brandenburg Gate and sent it off to Transylvania. Ten days later, Stokes Chesney rang the bell at Mrs. Kleinzach's.

"Oh, for God's sake," thought Dora. But Stokes said he was just stopping in on his way to Bremerhaven; he was taking the boat home tomorrow.

Dora had to admit he'd altered for the better in Transylvania. His dress and manners were more distinguished, European-like, and he'd grown leaner, less soft. Dora could have sworn he'd grown a couple of inches. Very sweetly, he allowed Mrs. Kleinzach to inspect and interrogate him for a quarter of an hour, and then he invited Dora to come out and have an ice cream with him. He appeared eager to get her alone.

"You seem a little sad," Dora said.

"Well, things are a bit of a mess at home. My father's ill."

"I'm sorry."

"Well, he hasn't really been well in a while, but you know how it is, when everyone depends on someone, it's like they'll be there forever. And then my brother Natty was supposed to be taking over for him, running the factory back in Melmouth, but that's not going so well. He's not so good with figures, or with people, especially union stewards. Anyway, that's why I've left Transylvania in such a hurry."

"You meant to stay a lot longer, didn't you?"

"It's just as well I didn't. I was starting to realize how stupid the whole question of theism is, anyway. I mean, even if there is a God, it's pretty obvious he doesn't give a damn about any of us. I've realized whatever it was that made us just left us here on this planet to shift for ourselves. And if that's the way it is, I'd rather face it head on than waste my time on all that supernatural non-sense.

"No offense," he added quickly, after a beat.

He put his hand over hers, smiling.

"I missed you," he said. "Now I know why you stopped writing back. I guess you weren't getting my letters if you were over here!"

"I did like the ones I got," said Dora. "I'll bet you write really good sermons."

"Well, they're a bit . . . stilted. Spoken words don't come as easily as written ones to me. I don't like talking in front of people that much. I'm really terribly shy."

Stokes walked her home. Dora felt a little sick from the ice cream.

"I think this place suits you," said Stokes. "You do look . . . so Germanic, so delicate, like a little Rhine maiden."

"That's what everybody says!" said Dora, smoking and frowning.

"Oh, Dora. Do you like it here? How long will you stay?"

"I don't know. Elise has been working in the movies, you know."

"Really!"

"Just silent ones. They don't have talkies over here yet. Just as well. Her German's still a little cute."

"Good old Elise. Well, I wish her the best. Tell her to take good care of you!"

*   *   *

When Elise came down for breakfast she found Mrs. Kleinzach mopping up under the dining table and crying. On the table was a cup of coffee and a roll, Dora's breakfast, untasted.

"It seems our little girl's in the family way," said Mrs. Kleinzach, losing a tear in her wash water.

Sick with misery, Elise fell to her knees, as if to help her clean up the mess, but too weak to do anything.

"You didn't know, did you?" Mrs. Kleinzach said. "Then you wouldn't know if it was that little American boy who came by."

"Oh, no, that's impossible."

"He didn't look very strong, that boy. But then Felix. . . . " Mrs. Kleinzach started to weep again. Elise gently took the rag from under her hand and went to get a fresh bucket of water. Mrs. Kleinzach followed her to the sink, washed her hands and blotted her face with a dishtowel.

Dora emerged from the toilet down the hall. "Go up to bed, darling," Mrs. Kleinzach told her. "We'll bring you something to settle your tummy."

Elise listened for the heavy patter of Dora's feet going up the stairs. Then she said softly, "You think it was Felix?"

Mrs. Kleinzach nodded.

"I caught him in the garden once," she said, "staring up at her window like a cat. In the middle of the night! He's a strange boy. Ever since his mother died. . . . "

She recollected herself, set down the dishcloth and reached for her handkerchief.

"Last year," she said, "he was touring in Bavaria, and he was very sick, we hadn't known. He collapsed, right on the stage. We had to put him in a sanitarium. Then we brought him home and tried to look after him, though it's not easy, with the life he leads. . . . He's a sweet little fellow. But he's more like a child than a grown man. If he's with the wrong people, it's very bad for him."

"It's my fault," said Elise. "I should have taken better care of Dora. I guess we'd better stay here now . . . not HERE," she added quickly, "I mean someplace in the country, maybe, till the baby comes."

"Ohhhh, no," said Mrs. Kleinzach. "Why should she go through all that suffering just to make one more brat for the Jewish orphanages? We'll take care of this quietly. There's an old friend of Dr. Kleinzach's, a professor at the medical college I can take her to. Little Dora will be good as new."

She made up a pretty little plate with some cut-up pieces of bread. "If she gnaws on this, it'll settle her stomach," she told Elise. "Go on, take it up to her."

Dora was lying on her bed, looking as though she was concentrating very hard on not being sick again. Elise set the snack aside and snuggled down next to her, gently laying her hand on Dora's stomach to warm it a little. Dora put her hand on hers gratefully.

"Well, this is pretty terrible," said Elise. "I'm sorry, Dora."

"I could die, I'm so ashamed," said Dora.

"No, now don't take on like that. We'll just take care of this here and then go back home, that's all."

"What about your soul?"

"'s okay," said Elise. "I'll get work in America. I can use my voice there. I can do radio, maybe picture work too. I could go to Hollywood—"

"Ucchh."

"The Barrymores did it."

"They're all drunks."

"The best people are doing it and nobody thinks the less of them. Everybody needs money. We'll stop home on the way there and take Turandot with us."

"Turandot!" said Dora, and started to cry.

"Oh, yes, you'll get your doggie. You'll get everything you need, I promise."

*   *   *

When Mrs. Kleinzach described Dora's symptoms to him, the Professor said he'd see her right away, that evening if possible. "The earlier you catch it, the easier it is," he said. "Don't give her any dinner and make sure she dresses warmly."

They met him at seven at his clinic, which was within walking distance of the medical college. He had very handsome living quarters on the floor above; the maid gave Elise and Mrs. Kleinzach tea there while they waited.

"Felix came to see Dora last night," Mrs. Kleinzach told Elise when they were alone. "I sent him away."

"Does he know?"

"I didn't ask him. Even if he did know, there's nothing he could do for her. He's got no money, and as far as marriage is concerned, thank God, he's in too deep with that woman of his to have anybody else. He hasn't admitted it yet, but I hear she's got him living with her now. 'The Dragon,' is what they call her. Her people own Tiedrich's department store. She's the real reason he's gotten on so quickly with his acting. She introduced him to everybody on the Kurfürstendamm, and now she's getting him into Ufa. So you see how it is. Well, they take care of their own, those people."

She drew closer as she lowered her voice.

"Do you know what happened when my brother married Felix's mother? Her people turned against them. Wouldn't see them. They told my brother, 'What you're doing is murder.' Because any children she had with him wouldn't be Jewish, and so they'd be dead, to them. What do you do with people like that?"

The Professor came upstairs. "She's ready to go home," he said. "I'll call a cab for you."

"Poor little thing," said Mrs. Kleinzach. "Did she cry?"

"No, she fainted fairly early on, so she hardly felt a thing. Let her lie on the couch for a couple of days, and keep her quiet. She shouldn't go upstairs or sit in the bathtub for at least a week. The most important thing is keep an eye on her! She's a ripe little apple, that's for sure. Marry her off as fast as you can. At least she won't be your problem!"

*   *   *

The kindly Professor had given Dora a powder to take (not morphine, he assured Elise) to ease the soreness of her little insides. So for the next few days she dozed on the couch in the parlor, with Elise in constant attendance, giving her fresh hot compresses and reading to her from Mrs. Kleinzach's treasured edition of "Faust." "I don't understand half of this," said Elise.

"It's beautiful anyway," said Dora.

It had been a sour, miserable business, an appropriate climax to the life she'd lived so far. Dora understood completely Felix's surrender to Morpheus, and would have gladly joined him, only Elise had told her to forget it, after her powder ran out she wasn't getting anything stronger than aspirin. Out of her mind as she was with the drug, which didn't take away the agony in her vitals as much as make her too exquisitely relaxed to care, Dora thought she glimpsed now and then the beautiful spirit of the little homunculus she'd carried for only a few weeks, who'd wanted her for a mother, and Felix for a father, God knows why, but had been turned away for his presumption.

Don't worry, she told him—she knew it was *him*. Some other time, I'll send for you again. Just not now . . . you see how impossible it is. And the little soul said, yes, Mutti, I understand.

In this way, Dora came to feel peace and a contented sense of motherhood deferred that eased and steadied her much as the Professor's powder did.

*   *   *

Mrs. Kleinzach stood at the foot of the staircase in tears as the girls brought down their bags to go home. There were three stout cardboard boxes waiting on the stoop. "From Mr. Süss to your uncle," she said.

They'd totally forgotten the books, the reason they'd come here. "They're so heavy," said Mrs. Kleinzach. "Let the cabman load them in the taxi when it comes, don't try to lift them yourself."

She ended up going with them all the way to the docks, even getting on the boat with them. She gave them chocolate and fruit and kissed them, crying all the time. The girls had to walk her back down the gangplank at the last minute, or she would have ignored the warnings altogether and sailed to New York with them.

"I think she thinks we're going to sink," said Elise.

"I wouldn't worry," said Dora, "I don't think she's got second sight."

Of course, the first thing they did back in their cabin was look at the books. The ones on top were cheap popular editions of Schiller and Heine and so on. A little digging below these top layers, however, revealed something interesting. Although these books nearer the bottom wore the same undistinguished paper jackets as the ones on top, browsing revealed that the book's jackets were not always matched to their contents, which proved to be of a a far richer and more eclectic nature. Most were in German, some in French and English, and two of them had long passages in Latin. The ones with illustrations, of course, drew their attention most. "I thought so," said Elise.

"You *knew*?"

"I guessed. You can see your uncle wouldn't want this to go

through the mail. He must have figured we could get away with walking them through customs. If you're scared we could always throw them over the side."

"Never! Look, *Ulysses*! First printing!"

"They must be worth a ton of money. No wonder Mr. Süss was so nice to us."

"They're going to take one look at me at customs and know just what's in there."

"Oh, no, they won't. You're going to have an acting lesson."

*   *   *

One of the stewards brought them a little note on a tray, just like in the movies. It was from Stokes Chesney, inviting them to have dinner with him in first class. "Lucky we've got the clothes!" said Elise.

"What's he doing on this boat?" said Dora. "He was supposed to be back with his family in Melmouth by now."

It turned out that not long after having ice cream with Dora Stokes had been overcome by terrible pains in his tummy, so suddenly that he'd fallen down right in the middle of Unter den Linden. Luckily a pair of nurses from an excellent private hospital happened to be passing by, and they'd taken him directly to their employer, who performed a first-rate appendectomy. "And what luck, he said that a sea voyage would be the best thing for me," said Stokes. Though his recovery was coming along well, he still looked delicate and becomingly wan, almost romantic.

"I'd like to come visit you. It's probably more fun down in tourist," said Stokes, "but I'd probably better stay put up here. I know I'm not the most exciting company, since I've basically just been vivisected, but I really would love it if you'd come up here and spend as much time with me as you liked. You could have your meals with me, my treat of course. What do you like to do when you're on board ship?"

"Nothing much," said Dora, "just read."

"I should have thought of that myself. All I've got with me is theological treatises. I don't suppose you've got any good books you could lend me?"

Dora couldn't help giggling like an idiot, which set Elise off too, and there was Stokes in his deck chair, beaming between them as though he'd just been named the wittiest man on two continents.

Chapter 13

Elise hadn't seen Dora so sad since last New Years. "What's the matter, baby?"

"Stokes wants to marry me."

She showed Elise the ring.

"Oooh," said Elise. "He really does!"

"I didn't say I'd marry him. But he asked me to wear it, to try it for size. He said it's not binding."

"You shouldn't have taken it."

"He made me. He can be really pushy. He said he bought it for me unter den Linden. He would have given it to me that day he came to visit, but he was afraid he'd frighten me."

"Are you frightened now?"

"Frankly, yes! What's he so interested in? It's just *me*!"

"I suppose we *should* find out some more about him before you go and marry him. But I have a feeling he's on the level. Look at that ring. That's the real stuff all right. You know how much this must have cost?"

"Just a stupid rock," said Dora. "Why's it mean so much to people? Does it make my hand so different to wear this thing?"

"You'd be surprised," said Elise.

"Well, I won't marry him if he makes me live in Melmouth."

"Why not?"

"It'd be horrible, I'd be bored out of my skull. I've lived in the city all my life. How could I go to some little village full of prissy Puritans who've never read a good book in their lives? I want to live in a real place with culture and a symphony and theater, and people I can talk to who'll listen to me."

"You wouldn't be far from Boston."

"The hell with Boston! They ban everything that's interesting."

"You could always visit me. It's not that far to New York."

"Oh, I will. In fact I'll make that a condition. And if he wants to keep me, he'll have to settle me there permanently in a house on the Hudson. With room for you *and* me."

"I'll probably have my own house out there. We could have adjoining properties."

"Why? Just live with us."

"I don't think Stokes would like that."

"He's always talking about collectives and communal living."

"Well, I need a place of my own. To work in."

"Yes, I guess you'd need a quiet place to work. You could have separate quarters, like a little Trianon with a studio. Soundproof walls, like a talking picture studio. But why buy a whole separate property with lawns and gardens to keep up, and a kitchen and pots and pans, and a cook and a washing machine, and a telephone? We'd probably be on the same party line anyway."

"What if I got married?"

"Well, I wouldn't expect you to stay a spinster just because of us. But then even if you had your own place, sometimes you'd want to stay over. What if you weren't able to buy the lot next door to us? You might even have to live in another town. No . . . living together makes much more sense."

*   *   *

Stokes was all for getting married right there on the ship. But the idea sent Dora into such a panic she started ducking the ship's captain whenever she saw him, as though for fear he'd ambush her and marry her to Stokes by force. Anyway, Elise thought Dora should at least meet his parents first.

"And he should have a chance to look at Mutti too," said Dora. "It's only fair."

"Besides, you'd think he'd want a church wedding, since he's a minister. He's going to be marrying all those people, you'd think he'd want to see what it's like himself."

"Oh, I don't want a wedding—I told him—all those people watching you, it would be horrible! I just want to do whatever we have to do to make it legal in the courthouse and get it out of the way!"

"I suppose you'd want to wait anyway, with his father being ill."

"That's right. He's got enough troubles now without *me*!"

*   *   *

There was some numinous quality in Stokes that made the customs men grow tender in his presence. All suspicion fled their minds, and they motioned him through the line with barely a squint at his possessions. The girls, however, got a more rigorous going-over. It was lucky they'd given the books to Stokes to carry through.

"I don't think I should be letting you go," said Stokes to Dora, as he put her and Elise into a taxi bound for Grand Central Station—he himself was headed for the Pennsylvania Station, and from there to Melmouth, Massachusetts, his home. "Will you come back to me?"

Dora started to cry—she felt so much like how she did last winter when she'd said goodbye to Turandot. Stokes there-thered her and sent her off with a fatherly kiss.

"What a lamb," said Elise, waving to him out the back window. "I'll make your wedding dress with lots and lots of of that shiny cream-color lace. It'll look beautiful, with your hair and his curls."

"You don't need to make me a special dress. I'll just wear that rose velvet I wore in *Der Lustknabe*."

"Hmm. I'll look it over and see if it's still in decent condition."

"It'll be just fine. A wedding dress is just another costume!"

"True. . . . What about your trousseau? You could use a new nightgown."

"I suppose so," said Dora, thinking what it would feel like wearing a gown you'd had morning sickness in on your wedding night.

"I can run you up a couple of things when we get home. We'll see about getting you some new stockings, too. Can't have you going to Melmouth looking like a little beggarmaid!"

Chapter 14

Though they put on a brave front for each other's benefit, the fact was that both girls dreaded their homecoming terribly. That they had in effect run away last January was bad enough, but Elise had quarrelled with her mother and not made it up with her before she left, breaking one of Mother's cardinal rules, which was to always part with a kiss, as one never knew when one would see one's loved ones again in this life. Dora had not only neglected to tell her Mutti and Opa where she was going, or that she and Elise intended to leave at all—the collusion with Uncle Ted had made her shy of discussing the matter—but had indulged in the shameful luxury of not writing a single letter home all the months they'd been gone. What would happen when they just showed up unannounced, under circumstances like this? Not that they dared to write or call ahead, for fear of being told they weren't wanted anymore.

Even though they'd treated their mothers unforgivably, they couldn't compound their heartlessness by never going home again. Indignant as Elise was at her mother's flagrant behavior in taking up with her father again, she still missed her. She wanted to see her so much in fact that by the time she got off the train she couldn't even wait for the bus, but literally ran home. Mother was so relieved to see her little one alive and evidently still respectable that she couldn't manage a word of reproach. They had a peaceful and satisfying reunion.

Dora certainly loved her own Mutti and wished her the best,

but that didn't mean she wanted to see her. At any rate, it was a great relief to her as she came up to the house to see her chief fear allayed: there on the front walk was Turandot, plump and glossy and lolling in an attitude of contented abandon in the mild morning sun. Sitting near her on the porch steps were a little boy and a little girl who were total strangers to Dora.

Children weren't in the habit of stopping by Dora's house, just as Turandot wasn't in the habit of going out of the house unleashed. Dora was amazed, and approached warily. Turandot must have heard her heavy footfalls from the sidewalk. The little animal shook herself out of her sun-drugged stupor and ran across the lawn, barking and wriggling in a wild hula of greeting. Dora danced back at her. The children squealed in laughter.

A woman in a blue housedress with the most beautiful wheat-blonde hair Dora had ever seen appeared behind the screen door. Dora felt the odd sensation of being looked at as a stranger from inside her own house. Was this still her house? But this was her dog, and Opa's name was still on the mailbox.

"Hello," she said to the woman in the door, "I'm Dora. I just got home." But this didn't seem to mean anything to the woman or children, and when she thought about it it didn't make much sense to Dora, either.

The children were in her way, and she felt gingerly about stepping over them to get to the door. But she couldn't just stand there. Like a little child lost and afraid to stray further, she stayed where she was and called "Opa!" It seemed more sensible than calling for Mutti.

Opa still had pretty good hearing; he tottered up to the door and said, "Oh, for God's sake, is that my little Doralein? Let her in, Hanna!"

"Opa!" cried Dora, and clambered over the children, followed by Turandot, all in a rush to see him again. "Forgive me, my darling!" she cried, forgetting her English and thinking and speaking in German again. Which was fine with Opa, who preferred German anyway, and also with Hanna and little Karol and

Bozena, who had just arrived from Galicia not long ago and spoke negligible English but knew three other languages well, including German, which they spoke in accents reminiscent of Felix's.

Though she'd feared for Turandot's well-being while she was gone, Dora had also felt some self-reproach for leaving Opa all alone with Mutti, not an easy thing to deal with at his age. But Opa just brushed away her apologies. "I knew my little bird would fly someday," he said, "I just didn't know how far!"

Apparently Elise's mother had told Dora's people where Dora and Elise had gone off to. They'd all been greatly relieved that the girls had gone back to the old country instead of New York. The fact that they had not only not returned in disgrace, but were movie stars after a fashion, and that Dora now wore a diamond on her left third finger eased their homecomings considerably. In times to come, Dora would never fail to wonder how once she'd let Stokes embed a bit of metal and rock in her flesh, people had become so much more impressed with her.

Dora was grateful that Mutti wasn't there, at least at first. But eventually she had to ask, and Opa gently told her that if she wanted to see her Mutti, she'd have to borrow Flivvy and take a long trip to the country, where the doctor had persuaded Opa to send her. It was a newly built institution with a first-rate young staff who were educated in all the latest methods of treating people like Mutti, whom the doctor had assured Opa would benefit greatly from a wholesome, well-ordered routine and firm but sympathetic supervision.

Of course this meant the old man would be left alone, with that big house to look after. So one of the ladies at Opa's church, who did social work with the Polish immigrants at the local settlement house, arranged for Hanna to come and stay with Opa as his housekeeper. So now Hanna and her little ones had a lovely home to stay in, and Opa had children's laughter and savory stuffed cabbage and meticulously ironed handkerchiefs to enjoy again, and Turandot got all the petting, fussing-over and table scraps she could possibly desire.

Naturally Dora's situation didn't seem real to her. When she had gone to the garage in the snowstorm last New Year's Eve to annihilate herself, she'd imagined, in her adolescent egotism, that her family couldn't possibly live without her. When she'd abandoned them a few weeks later, she'd thought again that those she'd left behind wouldn't last long. But to find that her dog and mother and Opa hadn't curled up and died, in fact were doing far better without her, made her think very differently about what her presence had meant in that household—that while she'd felt she'd been holding it together, she might in fact have been depressing it into total confusion, and by leaving she'd freed it to bounce back into resilient health again. *What's wrong with me?* she thought.

But there was the ring, that she couldn't stop fiddling with, drawing it back to see the shiny pink indentation it made in her finger-flesh. She wasn't homeless, far from it—Stokes would make her a home, wherever she asked him to. And she felt in her soul that that place was on the Hudson, as Elise had pointed out to her. Elise had warned her that her own struggle to win her rightful place in American theater would be strainful and exhausting. *But she didn't know that I need to be at her side through it all,* thought Dora. *I didn't know it myself. I thought I was weak and ridiculous, but now I can see I can stand quite a lot. In fact, I have more to give Elise than she herself understands. I'll never leave her alone again, that's for certain. And Mr. Stokes Chesney will just have to go along with us, or get left.*

*   *   *

The dreaded events were passed, the contraband literature had been retrieved from the train station by its owner (by mutual unspoken agreement, uncle and niece preferred to effect the delivery without meeting face to face) and Dora and Elise were testing Mutti's old sewing machine to see if it was still nimble enough to work on the delicate eggshell satin they'd chosen for

Dora to wear on her honeymoon night, when the telegram from Stokes arrived. It said FATHER IS GONE. PLEASE COME.

Father is gone. Dora couldn't help thinking how strange it was that for some people these words would come as a shock.

"Well, we'd better pack," said Elise, putting aside the satin. "I'll send this on to you later, I guess."

"No, bring it. Maybe we could do a little hand-stitching on it on the train."

"Dora," Elise said, "I won't be going with you."

"No?"

"Dora, three's a crowd. It's you he wants, not me."

"But you've got to come."

"No, I mustn't. I've got to go my own way for a while."

"Where will you be?"

"I'm not sure. I don't belong in Melmouth, I know that."

"Neither do I."

"You might be surprised. It might be the perfect place for you. Even without good books, if it's got the right people in it, you'll be all right."

"You can't make me go alone."

"Dora, you won't be alone, you're getting married. Stokes is the sort of man who's good for a woman. He'll make you happier than I ever would."

Dora threw herself into Elise's arms, so skilled at catching her.

"Dora, to be afraid . . . it's nothing to be afraid of. We've got to endure our going hence even as our coming hither."

She kissed her on the part in her hair.

"Ripeness is all," she told her. "And you're riper than you think."

Chapter 15

It couldn't have worked out better, from Stokes' point of view. The reason he'd tried to stampede Dora into a shipboard wedding was that he'd hoped to take her home to Melmouth and present her as his bride, a fait accompli. But as it happened the sudden decline and demise of his father muddied the family waters sufficiently for him to slip his dear girl into the other Chesneys' midst with as little resistance as he could have wished. In fact, the only person who displayed any class consciousness whatsoever about this pale, gentle little Midwestern interloper was Stokes' older brother Natty, the one who had been mucking things up at the shoe factory so badly since Father passed on. A plump, righteous Harvard business graduate with oiled-back hair like an otter's, he reacted to Dora's harsh-voweled accent and undebutantelike slouch by scowling and fixing his eyes somewhere to the left of her whenever she crossed his path, giving her a creepy feeling of invisibility. But Natty couldn't afford to do worse than that to Dora, as he desperately needed Stokes' near-sighted warmth and humane rhetoric to finesse negotiations with the shoemakers' union, or "the elves," as he liked to call them. Besides, in the larger scheme of things it didn't matter who Stokes married, as Natty's sons would inherit the larger portion, that is whenever Natty found circumstances propitious enough to produce them.

There is very little of Germany in New England, but as its

name implies there's a great deal of the British Isles. Whatever domestic instincts little Dora had were those of the Hausfrau, and so even such a civilized girl as she was found it strange to live in Melmouth, where the ladies drank tea with lemon and you were expected to keep your distance from the Irish, who did all your work for you. Nevertheless, there is that element of Old England in New England society that tolerates the nonconformist and cherishes the eccentric; after all, it did produce Stokes, not to mention his mother, who, now that her staid husband had crossed the bar, was becoming more of a bluestocking than ever.

A confirmed anti-Prohibitionist who presided over the local chapter of the League of Women Voters, she was very impressed by Dora's voracious reading habits, and thought that she ought to think about furthering her formal education, especially now, as her mind was still so young and receptive, and she wasn't yet occupied with tasks such as running her own household or raising children. Dora was flattered, and ashamed to confess that just the thought of entering a classroom again made her feel like putting her head between her knees. Mother (as she'd come to call her mother-in-law, Mrs. Chesney being a silly way to address her as she was also Mrs. Chesney, and Margaret just feeling far too familiar a way to address such a gracious lady) was so sweet to her and Dora was grateful for her good opinion. For this reason—and also out of consideration for the family finances, as it was expensive, and because of the Crash this was an era of necessary economy even in the Chesney household—Dora did not subscribe to *Variety*, and thus to her anxious regret was cut off from a potential source of information about Elise.

Wherever Elise was—and Dora hoped to God she was still somewhere on the surface of this planet, not underground or beneath the sea—she hadn't written, ever, not once, not to Dora or her own mother or anyone else. Dora asked Stokes if maybe she might hire a detective to track Elise down, just to make sure she was all right. "Now, Dora, of course she's all right," Stokes told her. "Elise is a smart girl, she can take care of herself. When she wants to be found, don't worry, you'll find her."

Dora's position in the Chesney household was really embarrassing. Though Mother treated Dora more like a good friend than a woman whose main purpose in being there was to have sexual intercourse with her son, Dora couldn't help feeling creepy about it. And naturally there was guilt too. The fact that Stokes was taking no precautions, and hadn't said a word to her about seeking them herself—assuming such a thing as a diaphragm or douchebag was obtainable in this solemn part of the world, had she even dared to try—made her wonder. Doesn't he ever think that I might have a baby? Or what if it's deliberate—what if he *wants* me to have a baby? What then, if I can't?

She didn't know what to think. On one hand there was precedent to believe that she could be gotten with child, on just the slightest provocation. On the other hand, wouldn't it serve her right if she couldn't anymore? But the Professor had been no quack—he'd seemed deft and sure, and all had been intimidatingly sterile. Just as he'd predicted, her insides had healed quickly, and gone about their usual periodic business just as before. She'd heard of women who'd actually gone back and had it done six or seven times. Which told you something right there.

It could have nothing to do with her. It might be Stokes, or something she was eating, or just her state of mind. If only she had access to Uncle Ted's library, with its wealth of frank and reliable information. The only thing the Melmouth public library was good for was letting the whole town know what you were reading. Fortunately, her late father-in-law had left something to soothe and enrich her querulous mind.

Though the others plainly felt at liberty now that the senior Mr. Chesney was gone, for Dora the old gentleman's presence was tangible, and she moved cautiously in his newly vacated environs, aware she was trespassing outside her caste, respectful of the color of his lingering aura and not wanting to outrage his spirit by seeming too much at home. One day, however, she ventured into his study looking for something to write with, and found his small but rich selection of books. All books being Dora's particular friends, she could not help but stop and converse with them. One titled *Extraordinary Popular Delusions and the Madness of Crowds* enticed itself into her hands. She read it with wonder, returning to it many times during those quiet years in Melmouth. It explained so much, and posed questions she'd never thought to ask.

*   *   *

And so Dora passed her days of legal concubinage, improving her mind and campaigning for Roosevelt with Mother by day, serving her master by night. Then there was the unprecedented evening when Stokes came home early, said that he and Natty had just gone over the books and it looked like the dear old shoe factory might just make a profit that quarter after all, and to celebrate he'd given himself the afternoon off. Did Dora want to take in a movie before supper?

"Strange how things have worked out for us," Stokes said as they strolled towards the theater. "I've meant to tell you so many times how sorry I am it's been like this. We really haven't seen much of each other in the daylight. I mean, I haven't had much of a chance to be a husband to you. In the sense of—well, you know. Having dinner together, that sort of thing."

"I'm very happy," said Dora.

"I never intended you to have to live this way. You were born to be more than a businessman's wife. I thought you and I could leave behind all that bourgeoiserie and get into the real life, out among the people. Like it was back when I was at the First Unitarian—every day a new point of view: artists, teachers, people who thought about ideas, not just figures and numbers and dollars."

"Your work's important," said Dora. "Everybody needs shoes."

"I don't like making money off other people's labor."

"They don't mind. They're making money too."

"Not enough."

"If you paid them more you couldn't make a profit and then you couldn't keep the factory going. You're already not taking a salary, what else can you do?"

"If I didn't have that money in trust I couldn't afford to go without salary. Oh, here I am talking about damn finances again. I'm sorry, my darling. Look, they've got nonpareils. Yummers. I'll get you a box if you promise you'll eat every one!"

It was in that theater that they saw Elise. She was only on screen during one sequence, and since it wasn't a featured role she wasn't in the credits. They had to sit through the whole program again to make sure it was absolutely her.

"Still in films!" said Stokes. "My my. That wasn't what she wanted, was it?"

"I knew that was where she was," murmured Dora. "She didn't want us to know."

She didn't say anything else all the way home. Stokes kept quiet, not wanting to be impolitic. Finally, however, he had to say it. He waited till they were in their room. "You want to go see her, don't you?"

"How can I?" said Dora helplessly.

"I'll give you whatever you need and you'll go."

He held her to his chest, blotting her tears with his sleeve.

"You will come back to me, Dora?"

Chapter 16

It's not hard at all to find a professional American actress; you just find out who her agent is and wait in his office till she turns up. Neither the receptionist nor other onlookers paid much attention to Elise and Dora's reunion; they'd seen most everything, and this was rather tame.

Of course they'd changed. Last time they'd seen each other they'd still been little girls. Now, in form, voice and deportment, they were entirely womanly. With so much love and leisure, Dora had grown curvy and rosy, while something in this desert life of hers had made Elise leaner, her eyes sharper.

"Stokes has taken good care of you," said Elise. "Where are you staying?"

"Chateau Marmont."

Elise moved right in with her, so that's where they stayed, at first.

It wasn't hard bringing Elise up to date on what she'd been doing all this time, as Dora'd been doing so little. Elise, on the other hand, seemed a little cagey about her own recent history. "When did you come out to Hollywood?" Dora asked.

"Not long after you went to Melmouth. You went east, I went west. I had more of a ways to go than you did."

"So you came straight to Los Angeles?"

"Nearly. I got off at Pasadena."

"I wish you'd of let me know."

"You know how I am about writing. And I didn't want to bother you knowing you were setting up a home, getting to know each other."

"Hardly," said Dora. "But what have you been DOING?"

She wanted an accounting, an explanation, of what Elise had been up to that was so damned important that she, Dora, had been tossed on the shelf like the Velveteen Rabbit to rot while Elise had been doing it. Living among reasonable people had unaccustomed Dora to Elise's infuriating elisions of logic, her way of spinning reality into the merest wisp of a story.

"If I tell you, you'll think I'm crazy," said Elise.

"I will not. You know I never do."

She sat in her creamy satin nightgown, the one Elise had made for her wedding night so long ago, sliding a toe through a bit of lace that had loosened itself from the hem, as Elise unfolded the story of her train journey west, through Indian country.

One evening while winding its way through the eerie desert hills, the train had stopped for a couple of hours at a station at the foot of an old pueblo. It had been a long, hot ride, and Elise had been grateful for the chance to cool off and stretch her legs. There were Indians selling blankets and so on. The work of one particular weaver was especially good, and Elise found some of the designs so beautiful and fascinating she looked them all over, wishing she had the money to buy them. There was one that particularly captivated her, a tapestry depicting wild dogs baying beneath the moon.

"You like the coyote?" the weaver asked her. Elise smiled and said yes. "I thought you did," said the weaver, smiling herself. "Come here a minute."

Elise thought she meant that she should follow her into the station, or someplace nearer than where she was leading, back to the pueblos carved into the desert rock, where the weaver lived with her people. It was dark and Elise felt the strange feeling we can't help having when we find ourselves surrounded by beings who are different from us, and might have a reason not to like us.

Still, she followed the weaver into her little cave-house, where from a secret place the woman brought out a sort of strap, like a belt. It was made out of real animal skin, all of one piece; you could see how the skin had been crudely cured so that it still held the coarse, luxuriant blond fur, intact as though still part of a living mammal.

"Would you like this?" asked the weaver.

"Why yes," said Elise, "thank you." She thought it was a gift.

The weaver happily nodded and said, "I'll take the pearl."

She meant the pearl lavaliere, the one Dora had given Elise on her graduation day, which of course she was wearing, as she always did. "No," said Elise, "I'm sorry," and she went back to the station and got on her train. It was almost time to leave.

She heard a tapping at her window, and saw outside the weaver, motioning as though she had something to say. Elise opened the window and leaned down to hear her. A moment later she felt a jolt as the train pulled away, and the fragile chain around her neck snapped, and the weaver made some sort of gesture—waving her rudely on, Elise supposed, having snatched the thing she'd come after. But then as she indignantly settled back into her seat, ready to call the conductor and report the whole outrage, she felt under her hand the fur of that coyote belt, which the weaver had thrown in as payment for the bauble she'd appropriated.

"She knew I'd need it," said Elise. "I suppose it was a fair trade."

The pearl might have been useful, to pawn for a week's rent, but after that she'd have lost it anyway. Hollywood was the best place for a young theater artist at that time, all the money and the work in the world was there, but the competition and living conditions were savage, much worse than anything she'd encountered in New York, which had been before the Crash, of course. So she worked out her own way to get by, with the unexpected assistance of the Indian weaver's gift.

Elise stored what belongings she had in a locker at Union Station, which wasn't such a bad walk to the cluster of studios down on Santa Monica Boulevard, especially in the morning before the sun got strong. She'd have her coffee and read the trades at a little newsstand with a sympathetic proprietor, and then she'd go to whatever cattle calls or auditions were on for that day. Sometimes she'd have dinner with friends or have a date, or go to the theater if someone had an extra ticket or passed her in. After that, she'd go to the hills.

"I would hide my clothes somewhere," Elise told Dora, "since they'd fall off anyway, and I wanted to make sure they'd still be there in the morning. And I'd put on my coyote strap and off I'd go. The funny thing was, I never slept. As busy as I'd been all day, I could run all night in my other body and never get tired. It was as if the coyote slept while the woman went about her business, and then when the coyote took over, the woman went to sleep. They took turns using my protoplasm. But it was still me all the time."

Since she usually didn't get much of a chance to eat during the day, as human food had to be paid for and there was little enough money for that most days, she fed as well as she could at night. Never dogs or cats, Elise assured Dora, only wild things: mice, and gophers, and sometimes snakes. She scavenged a little here and there in the city, but there wasn't much to be found. Humans were fierce competition for anything edible that didn't need to be caught and killed.

There were other coyotes in territories bordering her own, but most were too shy to come as close to human habitation as she did. She was careful to keep a low profile and stay out of traps. When the moon was out and she needed to sing, she climbed well up into the foothills before making a sound; there were hunters that found you that way.

And then things got better. That part had come through, that Dora had seen her in at the movies. Plus that director was in town now, that one from Berlin who had wanted her to call when she'd learned a little more German. Well, now German wasn't so important, and he'd asked her to call his secretary for an appointment, which was coming up in two days. "And just look at my *hair*," said Elise.

"Not to fret," said Dora, "we'll get those nails taken care of, too. What's a good salon out here?"

Dora never did get a look at that coyote strap, although she did have a good idea where Elise kept it. In all the years that followed, she never once asked to see it, nor did she try to sneak a look herself. She was too terrified of the thing to go near it.

Chapter 17

Dora was not about to leave her friend without a home. For much less than it was costing them to stay at the Chateau Marmont she leased an adorable little garden apartment the color of an orange Necco wafer, fully furnished, and quite handy to Paramount Studios.

"You can always find lovely property in Hollywood," Elise said. "Especially where the writers live. They're always getting discouraged and moving back to New York."

"But you're not, Elise? After all you've been through here?"

Elise drooped her head on Dora's shoulder.

"It's the same every time I put myself in front of a camera," she said. "It sucks everything out of me. I'm so exhausted I can barely breathe by the end of the day."

"When you act you give so much of yourself."

"And I'm glad for the work, I really am. I told myself, maybe if I'm good enough and true enough and give it everything I possibly can I'll be able to grow something inside myself to fill that place where my soul used to be. And you know sometimes I feel it coming back. But every time it tries to put out a nub it gets sucked off by that camera. Who knows if it'll ever come back now? It's been cut off so often it might have died."

"But souls don't die, Elise."

Elise squeezed her hand. "You're right," she said. "It's probably wandering around somewhere looking for me. Maybe that's a good enough reason to stay in pictures. That's how you found me, after all."

And it's a good thing I did, Dora thought. The rather wild-looking Elise that Dora had first taken in at the Marmont quickly reverted to her glossy, self-possessed self under her friend's care. Not coincidentally, work started coming to her in more substantial and satisfying forms. Part of this was thanks to Dora's wardrobe; for the first time since they'd entered adolescence, the girls wore the same size, and the ladylike, understated Bostonian outfits Elise now borrowed to wear to auditions shocked many a casting director into picking her out of the frowzy herd. Soon, Elise was making enough money to buy chic little frocks of her own at Bullocks, and a second-hand runabout so that she and Dora were spared the discomfort of eternally changing trolleys in the sweltering sun or uneasy darkness. She also ordered a subscription to *Variety*, which is how Dora found out about Felix. All that time in Melmouth, she hadn't heard a peep about his going into the movies, let alone becoming an international star. Of course, the film that had made his name had been banned in Boston.

From what she could put together from *Variety*, it seemed to have happened like this. Not long after she and Elise had slunk out of Berlin, the director Detlef Giese had plucked Felix out of the theater and put him in a film called *Der Doppelgänger*, about a tormented, lovelorn schoolboy (what else? thought Dora) who sells his shadow to a Mephistophelean mountebank, played by none other than Hermann Prinz (Berlin, though a great city, was really such a tiny town when it came to the arts.) Though critics denounced it as pornographic and a lurid throwback to Expressionism, it was a tremendous succes de scandal on the Continent, and even did well in England, where it was given the Certificate X. Here in America, however, even children were permitted to see it, in a circumspectly edited version titled *Uncanny*. In some markets it had done almost as well as the rerelease of *Frankenstein*, and *Variety* agreed with everyone who said that it was all because of the marvelous performance of Kurt Ross, who overshadowed even the great Prinz in his agonized intensity. Naturally, the buyers and sellers of talent in Hollywood had made inquiries as to Kurt Ross' availability, and Felix—who was known to all the world as Kurt now, completely and eternally—was rumored to be negotiating with representatives of Paramount. Whether he was still in Paris, where he had made a film with none other than the great Jouvet, or down the street from Dora and Elise at Paramount itself this very minute, *Variety* didn't make clear.

"He'd be an idiot not to sign," said Elise. "All the Jews in Germany are coming to Hollywood. The Nasties are chasing them out. Pretty soon there'll be more of them here than there."

"I didn't know Hermann Prinz was Jewish."

"He's not. Who says he is?"

"Well, he's here."

"Oh, my God. He is?"

He certainly was, and as a matter of fact was renting a house in Laurel Canyon, where he was getting together a little group of young actors for a master class. Elise at once called him up and asked if he'd take her. Delighted, he said yes, yes, yes!

This was how Dora ended up becoming the American dialect coach to the great Hermann Prinz. At first, he asked if she might meet with one of his newly arrived Austrian acting students a couple of times a week, just to chat with the girl and help her improve her English. The girl was smart and had a good ear, and when Prinz heard for himself how much more intelligible her English was, he asked Dora if she would have coffee with him on Monday, Wednesday, and Friday afternoons, and do the same for him.

"You have the most beautiful American accent," Prinz told her. "All the people who try to teach you English here have a very ugly kind of bourgeois Londoner sound in the way they speak. But when I listen to you speak English, I think you could have lived in California all your life. You have that 'twang,' that 'errrr.' When I can sound like that, when I can speak to the American people in their own language, I can be a star in Hollywood pictures again."

"Maybe you should practice with Elise," Dora said shyly.

Prinz made his usual delicious, growling laugh. "Elise!" he said. "Nobody could sound like Elise but Elise!"

My God! thought Dora, half fainting. He realizes! He knows! And then a joy rose in her, that she had never, ever known in all her life. Bad times were over now, or even if they weren't, they would never ever be as harsh or daunting. Because the time that she and Elise had lived for was coming fast, and soon. The exile in the wilderness would be over, and they would build their home on the river, together, at last.

Chapter 18

At first, Stokes barely even mentioned the topic of when Dora might come back to Melmouth. Eventually, he started sounding a little impatient, but Mother must have spoken to him about this, because he quickly changed his tactics, and actually managed to tear himself away from his shoemaking long enough to come out to Los Angeles and visit. "Dory-warry," he said one evening, as they sat together on the porch, watching the cars creak down the dusty street, "is this really where you want to live?"

"For now."

"I've told Natty I don't intend to stay with the factory the rest of my life. If we hire a decent honest manager, if we can find one, everything will go just as well as if we went on keeping it all in the family, rather better actually. I'd just as soon sell out, myself, but this isn't a good time. You understand."

"Of course I do."

"Now there's a possibility I could get a ministry out here. There's a fair amount of humanists, I'm told—"

"You'd do better if you did seances. Lot of goofballs around."

Stokes embraced and kissed her.

"Darling," he said, "you mustn't call them goofballs. They sincerely believe, and just because they're wrong doesn't make them any sillier than Catholics or Lutherans. "

He cuddled his arm around her shoulder.

"That's another question," he said. "Do you want me here?"

"You're my husband."

"But do you want me?"

Dora loosed her arm from where it was pinioned against his side, and slouched so she could hug him around his waist.

"Well," said Stokes, "if you really do I'll do what I can to tidy things up at home, and see about finding work here, then."

"No, don't. I mean, don't get a job."

"I wouldn't be able to give you a very posh life just on a gentleman's income! Of course I think I could find something a little better for you than this place. You'd want Elise to stay with us too, wouldn't you?"

Dora nodded.

"Thought so. Well, we'd have to stay pretty close to the studios, then. It's a shame. Seems like it would be so much cooler by the ocean."

"Lots of people live in Santa Monica. It's not far."

"Well, why don't I take a look around and talk to a few real estate people while I'm here. I wish I didn't have to leave, I'd like to just quit and stay here with you and Elise and the oranges."

"I know you can't."

"And I wish I could promise it'll be soon, but I will work on getting things straightened out back home. Meanwhile, I'll try to arrange things so that I can come back and see you . . . well, as often as I can."

"I'd like that."

"You're a funny little thing. You don't care much for money, do you? Neither do I. Must be one of the reasons I'm so fascinated with you I just can't stand the idea of not having you. In one way or another. Does that make sense? Probably not."

"Doesn't matter," said Dora.

*　*　*

So in a sense, Los Angeles was where the young Chesneys made their first home of their very own. Stokes came out to stay for a week or a few days here and there, and to make it a somewhat less depressing experience for himself purchased for his bride and her companion a perfectly lovely chalet-style property on one of the better canyons, which had formerly belonged to a screen siren whose brusque Mittel European intonations hadn't survived the talkies. In this place Dora had a setting chic enough in which to play hostess to her illustrious students, and they, in turn, started inviting their pretty teacher to gatherings of their own. Since it wasn't quite clear to some exactly what relation Elise was to Dora—they knew there was a husband or other that showed up occasionally, and yet the girls seemed so much like an old couple—Elise was often invited too, or welcome to crash.

It was while hobnobbing with the Hollywood Germans on the more exclusive end of the canyon that Elise and Dora were introduced to Mrs. Felix Ross, heir to Tiedrich's department store, otherwise known as the Dragon. She was a lovely Silesian Jewess with Slavic cheekbones and sparkling eyes, who drank rather more than she seemed to be used to and was the first person to leave the party.

Chapter 19

Elise noticed that Dora was starting to look a little odd and hollow-eyed, and was spending her mornings curled up in a little knot with Turandot on her stomach. Elise suspected the strange desert climate might be affecting Dora's delicate constitution, and so on her next free morning had Dora drive them out to the beach—try as she might, Elise still wasn't able to master the intricacies of clutch and gear shift, and was awfully glad Dora was so good at this.

Elise was just spreading their blanket on the pleasantly chilly sand and thinking "How salubrious," when Dora, shivering, seemed to gag on the salt air, lunged towards the water and threw up till the tears soaked her cheeks. She shuddered miserably as Elise washed her, bundled her in the softest blanket and laid her in the sand.

"Poor little thing," said Elise. "Well, wait till Stokes finds out. He'll be tickled to death."

Dora wheezed like a dying kitten, and then sobbed as though her heart would break. And then Elise understood everything.

"I honestly don't know how you arranged it," she said, when she could finally speak again. "Just like last time, I don't understand. I didn't even know you were seeing him! You must do it through pneumatic tubes or something."

Again, Dora wanted desperately to say she was sorry, or beg for understanding, but this situation was beyond such facile pleasantries. She huddled in the crushed ocean detritus, trying to warm herself in the meager morning sun while Elise stared at the surf and brooded.

"I guess it must be that there's a little half-Jewish, half-blond soul that wants to be in this world," she said finally, "and it's not going to let up on you and Felix till you have him. Is that it?"

"Must be," said Dora.

"Are you happy? Is this what you want?"

Dora thought hard. "No," she said. "But I might as well give in and get it over with."

The horrible sea sucked away at the sand near their feet. Elise realized the beach was no place for them after all, with this crashing noise, miserable dampness, and nauseating smells. She bundled up their things and helped Dora back to the car, where she drove them back to civilization for fresh milk and a nice warm bath.

The little dybbuk caused this gastric uproar just this once, to make himself known. For the rest of his residence inside Dora, he snuggled himself in a space where he would disturb neither heart nor stomach. Dora danced, played tennis, and showed little until the fourth month, when her little figure gracefully arched into a letter b. Her only anomalous symptom was a mild desire for orange soda pop.

"I've got to tell Stokes the truth," said Dora.

"Oh no you don't."

"What if I have a brown-eyed baby? Stokes and I have blue eyes. Brown eyes are dominant."

"There is such a thing as mutation. Anyway, dominance doesn't mean total dominance. You could have brown-eyed ancestors you don't know about. So could he. For all you know, Stokes could have Jews on his side."

"I doubt it," said Dora. "But you're right, he wouldn't necessarily know it wasn't his. Except if they did a blood test. . . "

It then occurred to her that blood types go on the birth certificate, and she panicked.

AR

"But they don't put *your* blood type on it," Elise said. "He probably doesn't even know his own."

She gave Dora a cigarette to calm her down.

"I suppose Felix doesn't know about this one, either?"

"God, no. God help me if the Dragon found out!"

"She must be used to this sort of thing by now. I wonder why she married him."

"He said marrying her was the only way he could get her over here, away from the Nasties."

"Good old Felix. Always looking out for the ladies. Well, I suppose they'll have kids of their own."

"I doubt it," said Dora. "She's awfully old."

Stokes preened with delight when he finally came and saw what a surprise Dora had for him in her pooching belly. The chronology of the little creature's origin didn't interest him in the least, or at least he never asked about it or why she'd put off telling him so long. He fondled it, kissed it and spoke to it as though he could see it straight through Dora's straining skin and tell that it was his very own boy. So that was all right.

Chapter 20

One day, as Dora drove Elise to work, Felix's face appeared above them in the sky, his skin a corpselike blue, eyes abulge, lips distorted in anguish. "Jeez!" said Elise. "They're gonna run somebody off the road with that thing up there!"

"Hideous!" said Dora. "They think it's going to sell tickets?"

Somebody did, but they were terribly wrong. Felix's American screen debut, *The Fiend* (adapted from Pushkin's "Queen of Spades," only they didn't use that title as it might be taken impolitely in the South) didn't make as much money as *Frankenstein* or even *The Invisible Man*. Still, Elise and Dora rather liked it. "It's probably over most people's heads," Elise said. "I thought Felix was a scream. Did you get that Lon Chaney thing he kept doing with his hands?"

"I wonder if the baby recognized his voice," said Dora.

"I wouldn't be surprised. I can't get that voice out of my head! He really picked up English fast. He didn't know a word when we knew him in Berlin, did he?"

"Oh, he'd had it in school. He just didn't think he knew it well enough to use it with us. God forbid we might laugh at him."

They drove in silence for a while, and passed another monstrous blue Felix. Elise said, "Oh, dear. Looks like they're trying to make him into another Lugosi. And look what happened to him. Poor guy."

"If only he could go back to Germany."

"Can't. Not till Hitler's out of office, anyway."

"Poor Felix."

"Well, as long as he's here they'll put him to work. He won't starve making horror pictures."

"It's not that. It's the dope."

"Oh," said Elise, remembering something she'd read in the morning paper about the crackdown on the narcotics trade. Anyone who got caught with dope or who even had needle marks in his arms was arrested, and doctors who prescribed for addicts got their licenses taken away. "Poor Felix!"

"I asked him once if he'd give some to me," said Dora.

"You didn't!"

"I did! He wouldn't, though. He said 'Dora, it's not for you. It's for people in pain.' I said, 'That's why you've got to give it to me!'"

She cried all the way to the studio, so hard that Elise wondered if the baby wasn't crying, too.

*   *   *

When he came out, Stokes Jr. looked just like a baby Felix smeared with raspberry jam and butter. But most babies look like Felix anyway, and when Dora saw the blue eyes she had hopes that the German in him would win out over the Jew. As genetics would have it, however, those beautiful eyes darkened to match the rich chocolate color of his true father's, and his hair came in a luxuriant chestnut brown, just like Felix's, straight as a pin.

"Lucky Stokey," Stokes Sr. said to him. "You don't have that silly curly girly stuff like Dah. Dark, manly fellow!"

"I think he looks like *you*, really," Dora told Elise. And that was the rumor that persisted, that Stokey was Elise's love child, raised in a tactful arrangement by the otherwise issueless Chesneys. As years passed, however, the growing resemblance to Felix was noted, and Stokey good-naturedly played along by learning to mimick the celebrated screen monster's funny Viennese accent. The matching timbre of his voice made the impression perfect.

Chapter 21

One night Dora saw the very devil. She was at one of those typical film business dinner parties where everybody goes straight from the table to the built-in screen in the drawing room. As they settled in she saw his tall, slim figure in grey mohair slip in and whisper to the host. He'd just come for the film, apparently. But it turned out to be a bad one, and Dora saw the chance to catch his wandering attention. Under cover of the weird, flickering darkness, she scooted around and stared at him as hard as she could, thinking, get up, get up. Finally he did; she gave Stokes her "going to the powder room" pat and followed him out.

"Well," said Drosselmeyer. "We've come up in the world, little girl."

"Mmhmph."

"And is your friend happy now she's got her soul back?"

"But she hasn't."

"I thought I gave it to her in Berlin."

"No. You wanted four thousand marks, and we didn't have it."

Drosselmeyer looked at her with weary condescention.

"Forgive me, you're right," he said. "Well, it's true Elise hasn't done anywhere near as well as she should have. It's a shame we never made that film in Astoria. It would have made all the difference to her career. That's the way it is with actresses. She's young. Maybe she'll find a good man like you did. Did someone tell me he's a bishop or something?"

"They don't have bishops in his church."

"Don't you belong to the same faith as your husband?"

"Oh, no, he's Unitarian. I'm a Theosophist."

"Another mixed marriage! They're hardly ever worth it."

He rubbed his beautiful, full lower lip.

"Theosophist! Like Madame Blavatsky? So you go to seances, and talk to the spirits?"

"All the time," said Dora, casually as possible, her heart doing a dip.

"They're all faked, of course."

"Only sometimes."

"How can you tell?"

"Well . . . you can't, if it's someone else acting as medium. But if it's you yourself who've got the spirit in you, talking through your own throat, then you know it's real all right."

"Can you make the spirits come to you, yourself?"

Dora breathed slowly, evenly, the way Elise had taught her, letting the oxygen flow to her bloodstream, steadying her nerves. "Sure," she said.

"Well, of course you would, if it's your religion. But it's strange to me that a girl as young as you would be interested in Theosophy."

"I went with my mother to sittings when I was a girl. That's where I went instead of church. It was nicer though, they were always at night and I got to sleep in Sunday mornings."

Drosselmeyer smiled upon her.

"Weren't you ever afraid of all those ghosts?" he asked.

"No, the spirits wouldn't hurt us. They're above that."

"That's very comforting."

Dora's instincts urged her to ask him then: "Have you ever been to a medium?"

"Oh, yes, I tried it, but they're all fakes, like Hanussen. You're the first real believer I've ever met."

Dora tried to look as pure and innocent as possible.

"Tell me," said Drosselmeyer, taking the bait, "could you

AR

really call to a person in the next world and make him come to you?"

"If I gave him a reason. If he knew I had someone he loved nearby."

Drosselmeyer swallowed. Briskly, he steered her out the French doors and into a little bower on the grounds where they wouldn't be seen from the house.

"Of course, a young girl would be the perfect medium," he said as they went, "with a body so frail, and a soul so delicate, she wouldn't offer much resistance to a ghost who wished to use her for his own purpose. There's the legend of the dybbuk, the ghost who takes up residence in the body of his mistress. Two souls in one body. That's what all lovers want."

"I guess," said Dora.

"Only some of us have too much within us, too much soul of our own, it crowds out everything else that we really want, and forces us to live alone. That's no good, at a time of life like mine. One longs for more than just one's work as a reason to go on living."

"Must be lonely, being a bachelor, out in the desert, an ocean away from home."

"I'm wondering . . . could we arrange a sitting? I'm not asking you personally, of course—"

"That's all right, I'd like to help."

"That's very generous. I trust you. I'd like it to be you. But I don't think your husband would approve."

"He's broad-minded, when it comes to religion I mean."

"You are a lucky woman. Could you come to my house tonight?"

"If it's not too far away."

"Just up the street."

"Oh, yes, the one with the broken flowerpots all over the roof."

Drosselmeyer snickered.

"Come with me now," he whispered.

"I couldn't do that."

"When can you come?"

"Midnight?" said Dora. She couldn't resist.

"Could you get your husband into bed that quickly?"

"Oh. This party . . . you're right. How late will you be up?"

"I won't be going to bed tonight."

"All right. I'll come when I can."

"Here's the address, in case you get lost."

He gave her a card, black cursive engraved on ivory linen stock, very boring compared to its Berlin counterpart.

"Is there anything you need?" he asked. "Is there anything I should do to get ready?"

"Just find a quiet room and tell everybody in the house to stay out of it, whatever happens."

He took her hand, bowed over it, and went back to the movie, which was still grinding away. Dora wandered through the house and found a stray highball glass, took a little of the watery bourbon on her tongue, and pondered the results.

Chapter 22

The Hollywood Drosselmeyer estate was a Spanish mission manqué, as ostentatious and silly as his Charlottenburg digs had been neat and chic. A trim Japanese houseman led Dora in. She missed the creaky old German lady at Drosselmeyer's old place.

Drosselmeyer came to greet her in the foyer. He had dressed to meet the spirits in a sort of black tennis outfit. "Can I get you anything, can I help in any way?" he asked eagerly.

"I'm fine," Dora assured him.

He led her down a corridor to a door which he unlocked. He turned on the light. Dora saw the reels and dangling celluloid strips and realized this must be the place where Drosselmeyer edited his films.

"It's not the most comfortable room in the house," he said, "but it's the quietest. I've got guests upstairs; they won't hear us, we won't hear them; it's soundproofed."

Most of the room was taken up with various platforms and cranks and machinery, but there was a corner with a little daybed covered with one of those rough hand-woven Mexican rainbow blankets. "That's where I do most of my thinking," said Drosselmeyer. "It's very comfortable. Why don't you sit there, and I'll pull up this chair."

"You may sit next to me."

"If it wouldn't disturb you," he said cautiously.

They sat together on the bed, a decent distance apart.

"Should I turn out the light?" he asked, getting up again.

"Isn't necessary."

He settled in again.

Dora had planned on asking him to join hands with her, but her palms were so wet she didn't dare. The words "vamp until ready" came to mind. Softly, she sang the first verse and chorus of "In the Garden." It went over well, he was smiling, but not mockingly, just as a man would smile when a pretty girl sang for him. Encouraged, she turned back the pages in her memory, and began reading at random: "May the spirits with us tonight enter in peace . . . in love and the spirit of fellowship, through our blessed Lord, amen."

"Amen," said Drosselmeyer.

"Now we call upon our guiding spirit to lift the veil between our world and the world we long to know, and join us, and let those beyond the veil know that we are here to welcome them, and to receive them in friendship and in love."

She next meant to silently slump forward like Mrs. Lelis always did, but instead to her shock felt her neck stiffen in a painful backward snap, and a sound came out: "UGH!"

Tonquish the Indian! She was terrified. She gasped through her open mouth, but the airway was full of something; she fell back, choking.

"Dora!"

It took her several minutes before the searing tightness in her throat relaxed enough to let her speak. Drosselmeyer looked terrified. "Was that the spirit inside you?" he asked.

"I guess."

"It's gone now?"

"I don't feel it."

"Could you make it come back?"

Dora burned with fright.

"Please," he said, grabbing her, "you must do this for me."

"No!"

"You said he wouldn't hurt you!"

She sprang for the door. He threw his arms around her but she slid out and sprinted, not remembering the way she came in, too panicked to think straight. She ended up outside in the garden, lost and stumbling among the stinging desert succulents. Drosselmeyer found her. "I'm sorry," he said, "forgive me."

There was real tenderness in his voice. "Little Dora!" he said, and led her inside.

Apparently the owner of this hidalgo (Drosselmeyer was leasing again) had installed a small soda fountain in the parlor for entertaining hungry young friends. Drosselmeyer sat her at the counter and made her a generous black and white sundae.

"I'd like to make you change your mind, you know," he said. "Will you let me?"

They smiled.

"What do you want?" he asked.

He'd said it. Joy overcame every other sensation. Marshmallow metamorphosed into ambrosia in her mouth.

"You know," she said.

Drosselmeyer wryly nodded and left the room. Dora clutched the cold fluted glass. The milky lotion inside was as warm as her palms by the time he came back with the can in his hands. "Do you know what it means for me to do this?" he asked.

Dora just stared at him. What a thing to say, she thought. As if this was HIS soul he had in there.

He opened the French doors and went out into the garden, a good distance away from the house. He opened the can and set it down on what looked like a bird bath or sun dial. Then he lit a match, holding it high over the can, then dropped it—and sprang away fast, as a flash and a roar erupted from the ignited test film. Dora's eyes snapped shut reflexively, but she still saw the burst of light inside her eyelids.

Drosselmeyer came out of the darkness, and closed the doors against the biting chemical smell. The flames had eaten up the film in one bite. No spark was left.

"Now your friend will be happy!" Drosselmeyer growled.

Dora blinked away the lingering ghost of the flame in her eyes. She felt her soul rise in triumph, and join with Elise's, dancing in freedom.

"Now sing your pretty song about the garden," he said, sitting next to her.

She told him to close his eyes, and took his hands in hers, and sang. Then, not sure what to do next, she stayed silent, a long time. She felt Drosselmeyer grow edgy, and knew she had him.

"Is anyone there?" he whispered impatiently.

Dora gave his hands a hard squeeze.

"Ah! Feels like a boy!" he murmured.

"You know it is," said Dora, in her deepest whisper.

"*Hansl?*"

She felt the spray of tears as Drosselmeyer, overcome, blurted out everything he'd been dying to say for so long but never dared. And it was easy knowing how to reply; the voice, it seemed, was not at all what Drosselmeyer needed, but to be heard himself, and more than that, to be felt. The irony of this communion coming to him by way of a female body wasn't lost on Drosselmeyer, but he wasn't ungrateful. He wept with gratitude to be allowed such liberties, with such conviction that Dora wondered if she herself wasn't a natural actress, like Elise.

He opened his eyes, saw her and shuddered a little. "He's still there?" he asked, not hopeful.

"Gone," said Dora, little and feminine.

No further ritual was necessary, and he'd broken the spell anyway by getting up and going beyond the fountain to get a soda water. "Do you remember anything, what happened?" he asked.

"Not a thing," said Dora. "I just went blank."

He wiped his lips, went to fetch her wrap, and walked her back to her car.

* * *

Stokes and the baby were sleeping. Dora changed into her nightie and went to Elise's room. There was just enough bed along Elise's back for Dora to nestle in, of course in the process waking Elise right up. "How do you feel?" Dora asked her.

"Ohh . . . wonderful," said Elise stickily.

"Really?"

"I was having a dream," said Elise. "It was a good one. But I lost track of it just now. How come you remember the bad ones and the good ones just evaporate?"

"The bad ones are full of neurosis. The good ones are wish fulfillment."

"If you say so. How come you're not sleeping with Stokes?"

"None of your business. Want to go to New York?"

"Yesssssss."

"You know Stokes'll stake you to any show you want to do."

"He's a prize, that man. I don't think you realize how good he is."

"I know, he's good and nice."

Elise offered her her own pillow, and scootched over to the other side of the bed.

"You'll have to start looking for properties," Dora said.

"I have one in mind. A good one. Listen. Remember that show I strangled in New Haven? The guy who wrote it's a genius, but he's fallen in with the wrong people, they think they understand him but they don't. They're trying to do him like typical drawing room Lunt stuff but it's not that pat. I think you have to do his stuff a little Gordon Craigy, a little German, you know."

"Felixian."

"Yeah, exactly, like that thing about the kids who went sex crazy. It reminded me so much of the one we did! Only we did it too light, it needed darkness and scariness. Because it's a scary play, and people love to be scared in the theater. That's why they go, really. Nothing's scarier than that space behind the back scenery. Because you never know what's coming out of it. And if all you've got in the stage is shadow . . . well, you've got them, because that's what they really come for. I think we need more of that in the theater. That's how we'll keep it alive. The movies are all light; that's what they are, just lights. The theater is *darkness*. Something that happens to you in the dark. And it's not just shadows in the lamp. It's real. That's what's terrifying about it. Real people in the dark, on the stage, in the seats, half crazy, half asleep; who knows what they'll all do next? I'm going to cable that playwright and have him meet me at the Algonquin in six days with all he's got. And tell Stokes to have his wallet ready."

Affectionately, Dora fondled the carnelian ring on Elise's left third finger.

You've got your soul back, she thought.

I do, don't I.